D0916909

The F*ck-it List

John Niven was born in Irvine, Ayrshire. He is the author of ten novels and has written for a wide range of publications, including a weekly column for the *Scottish Sunday Mail*. He lives in Buckinghamshire.

John Niven

The F*ck-it List

WILLIAM HEINEMANN: LONDON

3 5 7 9 10 8 6 4 2

William Heinemann
20 Vauxhall Bridge Road
London SW1V 2SA

William Heinemann is part of the Penguin Random House group of companies
whose addresses can be found at global.penguinrandomhouse.com.

First published by William Heinemann in 2020

www.penguin.co.uk

A CIP catalogue record for this book is available from the British Library.

ISBN 9780434023264 (Hardback)
ISBN 9780434023271 (Trade Paperback)

Typeset in 13.5/15.5pt Perpetua
by Integra Software Services Pvt. Ltd, Pondicherry

Printed and bound in Great Britain by Clays Ltd, Elcograf S.p.A.

Penguin Random House is committed to a sustainable future for
our business, our readers and our planet. This book is made from
Forest Stewardship Council® certified paper.

To Stephanie

Heartfelt thanks to my oldest friend Allan Carruthers for coming up with the concept of The List. I hope this acknowledgement is enough to ensure my absence from his. Here's to the next fifty years, AC.

America, 2026

ONE

'... usually, everyone asks the same question.'

'I see ...' Frank repeated.

This was not wholly unexpected. The dead and ruined ex-wives, the dead children. Some might say Frank Brill was an exceptionally unlucky man born at an especially unlucky juncture in history, a moment in the second half of the twentieth century where the America that had been, that could have been, was gone but still palpable. Like a kid staring at the aftermath of an iridescent soap-and-water bubble that had popped on the summer air, Frank could still feel the vapour, the sting, of the old America on his face. But still, here it was, the final insult. He almost felt like laughing, laughing at fate. *Fuck me? No — fuck you.*

A bright, cold November afternoon as Frank sat in the doctor's office in silence. Not quite silence — there was the soft hum of the computer on the desk, reminding Frank of cost, of the meter running. He didn't know the doctor well. Couldn't even recall his name at this second, though Frank was old enough to remember a time when you would have been able to, back when doctors made house calls. *'We'll get Doc Wood to come take a look at you,'* his mom would have said. Nowadays, in America, the only way a doctor would come to your house was if you were rich or already dead. And Frank was neither. This guy's practice had simply been on his HMO's approved list and close to his home.

The doctor moved a piece of paper on his desk and looked at Frank again, waiting. Frank looked out of the window, at the little courtyard garden, all bare and denuded here in the Midwest. There was a magnolia tree, the buds at the ends of the branches tiny and dead-looking. Come the early spring, come March, they would be swelling, soon to burst out into creamy-white flowers. Frank knew this because he had one in his garden at home. Sometimes it blossomed as early as mid-March, sometimes not until the second week of April. There were probably reasons for this, to do with the weather, how cold the winter had been and so forth. He'd ask Alexa, when he got home. Still, at his age, how sad it was to see things grow and not know how or why. All the flowers and trees he could not name. Would now never be able to name. There was so much stuff he thought he'd get around to knowing, just through some kind of osmotic ageing process. (*Osmotic* sending him back to tenth-grade biology, him and Robbie M tearing it up at the back of the class. Robbie in his 'Styx' T-shirt.) Like about carpentry, or electrics. The things old guys seemed to know about when you were a kid. But Frank had somehow missed all that stuff and kids today didn't seem to know it had

4

existed. What was the thing his daughter had tried to get him to use? 'Task' something. Task Bunny?

'OK,' Frank said. 'Thank you.' He got up.

'Ah, Mr Brill?'

Frank turning back, picking his overcoat up, already putting his tattered Colts baseball cap onto his head, covering his thinning grey hair. 'Yeah?'

'You must have some questions.'

'Nope.'

'We need to talk about treatment options.'

'No.' Frank sighed. 'We don't.'

The guy got up and came around the desk. He was young. Half Frank's age. Something to do with a ship. Bow. Bowden. That was it. Frank had known a Lizzie Bowden once, back in high school. You live long enough and everything has a resonance, an antecedent. Her tits, heavy against his ribcage as they danced to that song together, at the end of the night, at that party. Eighteen years old. What was the song? A ballad. A slow, end-of-the-night number. But, wait, Bowden was speaking.

'Look –' coming towards Frank, laying a hand on his shoulder, nervously. The kid had done this before, but not many times. 'Mr Brill, this reaction you're having? The whole "I'm not going to do anything" thing? It's much more common than you think. Most people, once they've got over the initial shock, once they talk it over with their loved ones, they realise it's wise to look at all the options.'

Task Rabbit! That was the thing. On her phone.

'I don't have any loved ones, Doc.'

Frank said this without self-pity or anger. It was just a plain statement of fact. *Good prose is like a windowpane.* One of Orwell's lines he'd always quoted to his junior reporters, urging them to keep it clean and clear.

'I'm sorry,' Bowden said.

Frank shrugged. What could you say? He wanted to make it a little easier for the guy. 'Look, son, don't worry about it. Shit happens.' In truth Frank was now fighting back an emotion the young doctor would likely have struggled to understand.

'Would you like the number of a counsellor? Someone to –'

'No. Thank you.' Frank tried to edge towards the door again.

'Mr Brill, Frank, I think you're in denial right now.'

'Why?'

'Why?'

'Why am I in denial?'

'Because, well, usually, everyone asks the same question.'

'You really want me to ask it, don't you?' Bowden just looked at him. Frank sighed again. 'OK. I'll play. Doc, how long have I got?'

'Well.' The kid swallowed. 'It's diff—'

'Yeah, yeah,' Frank said. 'It's difficult to say but it could be anything from X to Y depending on how aggressive it is and how much money we throw at it. Just … gimme a ballpark.'

'Without treatment? Maybe three to six months.'

'OK. I guess we'll just have to play it as it lays.'

'Play it as it lays?'

'Not a golfer then?'

'Every Time You Go Away'! That was it. It would have been, what? Senior year? 1984? Who the fuck sang that song?

And with that he was out through the reception area, past the concerned look of the receptionist, and into the cold wind of the parking lot.

Schilling, Indiana. Population 32,000.

The doctor's office was in a small retail park on the outskirts of town, where most things were now. There was a lawyers' (McRae, Dunbar & Wallace: *'all pro-bono work considered'*) and what used to be a real estate place, empty for a couple of years now, a sun-faded banner hanging down in its front window: *'IVANKA 2024! MAKE AMERICA GREATER!'* Just across the highway was a mini-mall: shoe store, nail salon, tanning place, an Olive Garden and a Subway, its foresty-green signage suggesting health food, which it probably was compared to the KFC next door, the one where Frank used to stop sometimes on his way home from work to pick up a bucket of chicken, back when he would have had use for a whole bucket. When there were other mouths. The passing traffic whooshed and churned the trash in the parking lot in front of the food places, paper napkins and cardboard boxes and soda cups and whatnot, chasing each other in dusty petrol fume circles. The newspaper's office, its final office, had been just east of here, further along the I–22. Was it still unoccupied? Boarded up? Frank hadn't driven by to check in months.

He stopped at the kerb to let a FedEx truck glide silently past him – electric, noiseless and driverless. The fucking things still freaked Frank out, Frank who clung to the old ways, who was even now fishing his car keys out of his pocket. Yeah, he guessed you couldn't argue with the actuarial tables that showed how automated cars caused far fewer accidents than those driven by people. He understood the logic, looking at the FedEx vehicle now, beeping an electronic warning as it reversed slowly and carefully into a parking bay across the lot. The CPU in the driverless car didn't speed because it was late, it didn't run stop signs, it didn't accelerate angrily behind other cars after they'd cut them up. The chips and sensors kept it in position on the road, within the speed limit and a safe distance from other vehicles. They were undoubtedly, provably, safer. Still, they freaked Frank out.

He sat down on a bench and watched the lunchtime traffic, his right foot thrumming up and down on the side-walk. *A drink*, went the reflexive thought. *I really want a drink*. Just as reflexively Frank's hand went into his pocket and he fingered the tiny plastic penguin. Thirteen years now. He breathed deeply for a moment or two and got past it. That emotion Frank had been fighting back? The one Dr Bowden would have struggled to understand? It was *excitement*. Because Frank had known for months he had cancer. The loss of appetite, the pains down there, the difficulties in the bathroom department. He'd been googling like a madman. Frank had always had an appetite for research and it had helped make him a good reporter. Just as, later, his organisational skills had helped make him a good editor. And, in the last few months, as he let the cancer grow inside him, welcoming it as you would an old, long-lost friend, he'd been using both of these skill sets, working tirelessly on the thing that had gradually grown into the stack of five files (pink, orange, green, yellow and red, ranked in order of imagined difficulty) that now sat on his dining-room table, next to his computer. And now, now that it was all nice and official, it was time to put that

research and organisation into practice. Frank was sixty.
He'd never been in trouble with the law his whole life.
Still, the day was here. He was dying. And soon. It was
official now:

Given everything he'd been through in the past few years,
Frank was no stranger to suicidal thoughts. Thoughts? Hell,
he'd been on the edge of bridges, in the bathtub with the
whiskey and the razor blades, in the garage with the
aluminum stepladder and the noose. He was no stranger
to imagining what the last thing he'd see would be: the
black water rushing up to meet him; the cork-tiled ceiling
of the bathroom as the warm water turned scarlet around
him in the tub; that can of old blue paint (*the boy's room*)
on the shelf next to his toolbox and the tyre chains, strobing
in and out as he dangled, spinning in circles as blood filled
his eyeballs. But he'd always been too chicken.

He wasn't going to chicken out of this.

Frank had had three wives and two children.

He didn't have any of them any more.

I don't have any loved ones, Doc.

He just had The List.

TWO

'It's a good living, son. Clean.'

He'd become a newspaper man because of his old man, Frank Senior. His dad had been a typesetter, throwing hot metal down at the printing plant on Coolidge Street. (Condominiums now. Two bedrooms starting from $195,000. No deposit required.) Frank Sr had learned his trade there as a boy. Got his start in the summer of '53, straight out of school. He'd been there thirty years by the time Frank was finishing high school and starting to look around for a job of his own. Frank had confided to his dad one night, out there on the porch with a couple of beers, at the old house on Hoover, that what he really wanted to do was become a writer. The old man had sucked his teeth and whistled. 'Gee, Frankie. I don't know. Seems like it might be tough to make money at that.' His dad had always been impressed with the guys who came down from the paper to check the layouts. The subs and the editor, Arnie Walker, an ex-marine, an Ike clone who edited the *Schilling Gazette* for over thirty years – from '46 to '77 – when the paper was the 'voice of the Tri-County area' and its circulation was over 200,000. Old Arnie dropped dead of a heart attack at his desk, a pork tenderloin sandwich in one hand and a half-subbed piece about a proposal to build a new freeway through protected land in the other.

Arnie and his boys would come down to the printing plant and make corrections and amendments and laugh and joke with the typesetters. But they wore shirts and ties instead of blue overalls. And their hands and fingernails weren't stained with thick black ink. And on Friday afternoons, after the Saturday paper – the last issue of the week – was put to bed, they'd all go over to Macy's Bar & Grill, just up ahead of where Frank was making a right now, grumbling at the traffic. If he'd kept on he'd have passed it. It was still a bar. Had changed its name to Barcadia in the late eighties, then to something else. Frank couldn't remember what it was called these days. At Macy's they'd get stood drinks by Brock Schmidt, the owner of the *Gazette*. They loosened their ties and had their three-Martini lunch and laughed and joked and pissed and moaned and talked about who wrote good copy and who was screwing who and whatnot and Frank's dad thought that looked like the good life right there all right. 'That's a way, you know. You could write and get paid to do it. It's a good living, son. Clean. I could have a word with Mr Walker.' Frank graduated high school in 1983 and strolled into the *Gazette* as an 'office boy', fetching coffee and sandwiches, running copy from one desk to another. Learning what made a good opening para. It was still a time of electric typewriters.

Of double-spaced A4 marked up with blue pencil. Of linotype racked up by men with burned, calloused hands. Bottles of Scotch in the sub-editors drawers. But, within a few years, those small boxes the colour of cigarette smoke with a little Apple on them started appearing on the desks. You could typeset right there on the screen.

Frank took the freeway out of town, heading for the western suburbs. He turned the radio on and got a news report, something about Vice President Hannity causing offence at the UN, refusing to apologise for America's policy in post-war Iran, where we were taking the oil. Reparations, how for every dead American troop we were going to take whatever. Frank punched the tuner and got the next station – Journey doing 'Don't Stop Believing', a song that had come out when he was in high school, that he'd heard so often now that it was about as surprising and interesting as hearing a recording of his own name being repeated over and over. But he left it there.

By the nineties, by the time Frank was deputy editor, the sound of clacking plastic keys had replaced the metallic chatter of the big Smith-Coronas and Frank's dad was out of the job he'd held for the duration of eight presidents.

Frank prospered though.

He had a good eye for a story, was diligent in his research and got along well with Mr Schmidt. He loved being part of a small band of men (and it was still all men back then) who were responsible for creating a newspaper out of nothing six days a week. He liked the pressure. Although some (his first wife Grace among them) would say that as he progressed up the ladder towards editor Frank acquired a hardness, a caustic veneer that came from an intelligent, sensitive man spending time with people tougher than him whose approval he sought. 'Baloney,' Frank says aloud now, just thinking about that diagnosis, as he makes a left onto Harding, his street.

A lower-middle-class street in the Midwest, lined with American linden trees. Driveways leading off to homes built between the late forties and the late sixties. From the GI Bill to the moon landing. A street for families, where bikes were propped against front porches and plastic toys were scattered around front yards, the aftermaths of battles abandoned due to dinner, or TV. Where kids were halfway down the street before they heard the screen door slam behind them. Frank had bought the place with Pippa, his third, his final, wife seventeen years ago, back in early 2009. His timing was good – the market had crashed just as the ink dried on his divorce from his second wife, Cheryl, and the three-bed, two-bath home was a steal. His timing was good, but that was about all. It turned out that in the end Frank would only need one bedroom and one bathroom. Back towards the end of his drinking days he'd often roam the rest of the house, tumbler of Scotch or gin in hand as he looked into the redundant rooms – just storage spaces now, cardboard boxes and plastic bags – imagining all the life and activity that might have been played out in them, the laughter and arguments they might have seen.

Often, when he pulled up in front of the house in the late afternoon, back from whatever errand had constituted his activity for the day, Frank would sigh as he looked up at the place and contemplated the evening unspooling ahead of him, the same one he'd been having for years now: the early evening bustle around the kitchen, maybe steaming some green beans or broccoli to go with his meal-for-one, a kind of concession to health, a self-delusion that he was actually doing some cooking. Then the long stretch of mid-evening, channel-surfing, reading, as the street gradually darkened outside. Then the long, pointless chats with Alexa, the arguments with God, the raging at the world, all gradually subsiding as tiredness finally overtook him and he fell asleep in the Barcalounger in front of the TV, the barely touched meal-for-one (carbonara, meatloaf, fish-in-sauce) on the little table beside him, the novel he'd read several times before (*Garp*, *Couples*, *The Sportswriter*) in his lap, the movie he'd seen dozens of times (*Jaws*, *Wall Street*, *Die Hard*) fizzling in front of him in the dark room, the half-drunk cup of herbal tea falling with a muffled thunk Frank did not hear into the carpet. He'd awaken, startled, in the early hours, disoriented, realising he was alone in his living room, a bar of street light coming through the gap in the curtains. But, tonight, as he climbed out of the car, Frank felt optimistic, almost cheerful for the first time in as long as he could remember. He had work to do.

He missed work. Editing a newspaper — even a small, regional paper like the *Gazette* — was like being a film director, Frank imagined. Every day there was urgency ... demands. You were being asked questions all the time. 'What about this?' 'What do you think of that?' 'Have you looked at this yet?' 'You need to ... we need to ... I need to ...' You were *needed*. And then he wasn't. Those small grey boxes. Frank had made editor in 2001, at the age of thirty-five. He got fifteen years in the job. As it turned out they were fifteen years of increasing budget cuts and firings and shrinking advertising revenues before the small grey boxes that had done for his father did for him too. Brock Schmidt – approaching seventy – sold the paper and retired down to West Palm Beach, just after Trump won his first term.

At the time Frank thought this was as bad as his life could get, a notion that now caused him to chuckle, to shake his head and emit a low whistle as he reflected on how idiotically he'd underestimated the savage fury of the universe. He was only forty-nine, with a new, younger wife and a four-year-old son. But he'd been there over thirty years, and at a senior level for most of it. His redundancy payment was generous.

Pippa had gone back to teaching and Frank had finally got the chance to work on his novel, i.e. he became a house husband. He went from being the bread-maker to buying a bread-maker. He learned the ways of focaccia and sour-dough and gained fifteen pounds. The bread-maker went into the garage. He spent time at the local library, doing research for a book he grandly imagined would be a history of social housing in Indiana. He stopped a few months later, after he'd amassed several legal pads full of notes, when he saw an old man at a nearby table. The man was filthy, clearly homeless, and he too had a stack of legal pads in front of him, full of notes for something he was working on, some grand key-to-all-mythologies. Frank walked by and glanced at a page over the man's shoulder. A paragraph read: '*The centre is all. The centre is held in place by the angels. The angels are ruled by the GOVERNING PRINCIPLE (see appendix 2). The GOVERNING PRINCIPLE is ...*' Frank now saw that the man had pieces of newspaper stuffed in his ears. He stopped going to the public library to work on his book after that.

So he got Adam ready for school in the mornings, he hit the golf course or the driving range, he shopped and prepared the evening meal, and he was there with a plate of carrot sticks, a glass of milk for Adam and a chilled glass of Pinot Grigio or Sauvignon for Pippa and a Diet Coke for him when the two of them came back in the door at 4.30 sharp. Pippa taught at Adam's school, Truman Elementary. (Yes, *that* Truman Elementary in Schilling, Indiana. You've got it now, haven't you? You've put the name of the school together with the names Pippa and Adam Brill and the dates and you know where this is going now, don't you?) Looking back on this period of his life a decade later Frank could only view it as a golden time, shot with gauze or Vaseline on the lens, shot by Tony Scott or Adrian Lyne (he'd fallen asleep in front of both *Top Gun* and *Fatal Attraction* this week), with everything soft and rich and smeared and sumptuous. But if he was being honest, and at this point there was no point in being anything else, he knew that at the time he'd been tortured by feelings of worthlessness and insecurity: here he was, an American male born in the 1960s, baking and going grocery shopping.

Another revelation of old age: life only has golden periods in the rear-view mirror. Upfront, through the windshield, it's panic and chaos as it all comes at you much too fast.

Frank came in through his front door, tossed his keys on the hall table, and shouted out, 'I'm home, Alexa.'

'Hello, Frank,' she said. 'How was your day?'

'I have cancer,' taking his coat off now.

'I'm sorry. I don't understand that, Frank.'

'Yeah, me neither. Lights.'

Alexa turned the lights on. She'd been a present, from his daughter. Frank felt like ... what? He felt like celebrating. Maybe he'd go out to eat later. He poured himself a Coke over ice in the kitchen and wandered across the hallway, where he stood in the doorway to the dining room, drumming his fingers on the door frame as he looked at the stack of files on the table, the inert PC, the plates and mugs and yellow legal pads. Sipping his drink, turning the computer on, Frank settled uncomfortably into a hardwood dining chair. He felt like he should have a toast to it, the cancer, all up in his asshole. It figured. Frank had given his typical American ass a fairly hard time all its life: red meat, chillies, jalapeños, fried chicken, pizzas and nicotine, all washed down with an Atlantic of liquor. He bore it no grudges. Decades of this and you'd throw the towel in too, wouldn't you? You'd say, 'Fuck me? *Fuck you. You* deal with this shit, buddy. I'm outta here.'

Frank remembered he had to transfer some money, from savings to checking, as he wanted to withdraw a bunch of cash tomorrow. He got the bank home page up onscreen and then realised he'd forgotten his password. Fucking passwords – how many did you need these days? Pippa helped him set it all up. Now where had he written them down? He turned around one of the framed photographs on his desk, one of him and Pippa and Adam, and there on the back of the frame, in his tiny, neat block-capitals printing, were all his passwords. (Pippa had scolded him about this. 'Gimme a break,' Frank said. 'What? Someone's gonna break in and know I've written my passwords on the back of this photo?') As he did his banking he noticed the date on the computer – November 11 – and suddenly remembered something else. 'Alexa,' Frank called over his shoulder, 'CNN.' He heard the set come to life behind him and he turned round to see the parade in Washington was in full flow.

Huge crowds were packed into the bleachers, waving their flags, cheering in their red MAGA and KAGA and MAG hats as they watched the soldiers and the hardware rumble past: tanks, howitzers, assault vehicles, rocket launchers, thousands of troops, all lumbering away from the White House, towards the Capitol. The lead tanks were huge, M1 Abrams battle tanks, each weighing sixty short tons. Soldiers stood up through the open hatches, rigidly saluting the podium. You could faintly hear the cheers in the background – 'USA! USA! USA! – as the camera swung over the rows of spectators. And here it was, the real America, the people who had travelled from Florida, from Nebraska, from Kentucky and, yes, from here, from Indiana, up to Washington, spending money they could ill afford to pay their respects on Veterans Day. They were cold and wet and mostly old and fat and they were all wrapped in thin, cheap coats, with their cardboard signs saying 'GOD BLESS THE TRUMPS', 'DEATH TO DEMOCRATS' and, 'LOCK HER UP'. (The last one increasingly puzzling to Frank as former Senator Clinton had died peacefully in her sleep three years ago. Perhaps they feared a ghost situation, a zombie Hillary, clawing her way out of the grave and trying to take their guns and delete more emails.)

There had been no tanks for the first few years. The roads couldn't handle it. One of Trump's first acts early in his second term had been to order a multi-billion-dollar programme to widen and strengthen Pennsylvania Avenue to accommodate the monsters every November. As Frank remembered this, as if on cue, the cameras cut to the presidential podium: President Trump and her husband Greg. (Her second husband, Jared, languishing in Rikers, having taken the fall for an awful lot of shit.) Vice President Hannity and his wife on her left, and on her right, still towering over the others even at eighty, Donald and his new wife, his fourth wife, Crystal, her belly swollen in the final trimester of her pregnancy. Thunder erupted suddenly as three of the fighter planes smashed through the sky above the parade. Trump put a protective hand on Ivanka's shoulder as he shouted into her ear over the jet roar, his finger jabbing into the sky. Ivanka wore a cream overcoat and fur hat, her father his trademark black overcoat and red tie. Trump looked down at the vast, cheering crowd and gave them his signature thumbs up. They went wild. It had been a masterstroke, you had to admit: firing Pence halfway through his second term and nominating Ivanka as VP before resigning the office due to ill health. Ivanka automatically became president and had eighteen months in the saddle before she had to fight an election. Obviously one of her first acts in office had been to pardon her father of the multitude of charges he faced.

'You wonder,' the CNN commentator sighed as the coverage switched to a shot of the aircraft thundering off into the distance over the Capitol, 'can we afford to have all these fighters and tanks here given the current situations in Iran and North Korea?' The aftermath of the wars, still going on, years after Trump stood on the tarmac in Tehran, in Seoul, and gave his victory speeches. The oil was already flowing from Iran. What the American people were going to get out of the post-nuclear moonscape of North Korea remained less clear.

'Alexa, Fox,' Frank said.

The channel changed. The shot of the jet fighters was pretty much the same, but the commentary went up a gear or three. 'OH WOW!' The female reporter was shouting over the noise. 'YOU GUYS SHOULD BE HERE! THAT WAS INCREDIBLE!'

'The new F-36s, Roberta . . .' the studio anchor said.

'That's right, Ken, the most advanced thing in the sky.'

The camera cut back to the Trumps, applauding on the podium. 'And there's Crystal,' Roberta said, 'looking absolutely *radiant* I have to say.' The former president's new wife of just over a year was saying something in Donald's ear. She was twenty-eight, Frank knew, just a few years older than Olivia would have been now. 'Don't they make a beautiful couple?' Roberta went on. The Donald, everyone agreed, had done an incredible job of getting over his grief following the death of Melania, who had perished in a helicopter crash just a few months after he left office, just after, rumour had it, she had signed a) divorce papers and b) an eight-figure book contract.

'And, Roberta, I think Crystal's wearing one of the president's designs, isn't she?'

'That's right, Ken. It's a pantsuit. They're available on the White House website as a matter of fa—'

'Alexa, turn the fucking thing off.'

'I'm sorry, Frank. I didn't unders—'

'TV OFF!'

The screen went black and the room was quiet again. The clock on the mantelpiece told him it was nearly 5 p.m., the street outside darkening swiftly as night fell. He should really try and eat something. He still had to pack. 'Alexa?' Frank said, thoughtful, expansive and philosophical even, as he swirled the Coke in his glass.

'Yes, Frank?'

'Why does God hate me?'

'I'm sorry, Frank. I don't understand that question.'

He looked at the row of bottles still in the liquor cabinet – furred and dusty with age – and the thought came to him again: *Why not? What could it possibly matter now?*

There had been a few fellow ex-drinkers in Frank's house over the years. They'd all done AA of course and had been amazed to see that Frank was sober and yet lived with all that booze right there, that he hadn't had his 'pouring it all down the sink' moment.

Frank didn't get this. It was there, it wasn't there – what did it matter? Did you really need that moment of drama at the kitchen sink? He could be down the liquor store and fill the trunk of the car in fifteen minutes. He'd decided not to drink again, and that was that. Having or not having booze in the house made no difference. Frank hadn't done AA. He'd just stopped. In lieu of the sobriety chip – the little metal button they gave you – he'd taken to carrying around the tiny penguin that had belonged to Adam. Pippa had taken it off the boy because it was too small, too easily swallowed, and Frank had found it on a shelf in the kitchen one afternoon. It helped him focus sometimes. He squeezed it between his thumb and forefinger again now as he took one last look at the bottles before turning out the light and heading for the door.

Frank's sobriety.

He'd grown up and worked in newspapers – a drinking culture. He'd stopped when he was forty-seven, when Adam was two. There had been no grand moment of clarity, no hitting bottom, just a gradual realisation of what this habit he'd had for nearly thirty years was costing him. He'd gone through periods of not drinking, a week or two here, a couple of months there, and had always slipped back. He'd noticed something: when he was drinking his working hours extended – staying late at the office, having a couple of whiskeys with the subs. Hitting the bar with the team after the paper had gone to bed. His social hours too – staying at the clubhouse that bit longer after his round of golf. At home, in the evenings, there'd often be a reason to be in his study for a while, reading, 'working', when he was really getting increasingly toasted, thinking his grand thoughts, fucking around on the internet. Then there would be the hangovers. They were rarely severe, rarely disabling, but often enough to make him grouchy and withdrawn. The truth was, when he was sober he delighted in spending time with his wife and son. When he was drinking his family became a minor inconvenience to him. As he approached fifty, conscious of the fact that Adam – toddling and talking now – was very likely going to be the last child he ever had, Frank decided that family was where the smart money lay. That day, at the grocery store, he'd bought a six-pack of diet sodas, and instead of opening some wine while he cooked that night, he poured himself a soft drink over ice and that had been that. Thirteen years sober now.

There had only been one lapse, which most people would have found entirely forgivable ...

THREE

'Many of the victims may not have died right away …'

Around lunchtime, a little over nine years ago now.

May 5, 2017.

A really beautiful day, in the high seventies. Frank had been in the high seventies too that morning: high-fiving himself in the locker room at Forest Glade, having shot a 78 to take the money in his Friday morning four-ball. He'd dropped Pippa and Adam at school at 8.30, been off the tee just after 9 and was strolling out of the shower by 1.04. (He remembered because he looked up at the digital clock above the doorway that led from the locker room to the clubhouse, already smelling grilled cheese wafting down the hallway from the dining room, thinking about having one and a root beer before heading home.)

Forest Glade was the most affordable private golf club in the Schilling area. Two divorces by the age of fifty had taken their toll and Frank could no longer afford the fees over at Crescent Heights, the country club he'd joined back in the early nineties. Married to Grace then. One wife and no children. Saturday morning golf with George, Al and Brad while Grace played tennis with the wives – Gina, Clio and ... Melanie? Mandy? Then lunch and cocktails by the pool in the summer. Twenty-five years ago. Whatever happened to all those guys? The lives we have, not singular. Several wrapped in one. The people who came into your orbit and then spun off, crossing your mind at Christmas, toiling over the card list, or when you came across an old photograph.

That May afternoon Frank had been towelling off in the locker room with two of the guys he'd just beaten – Art and Ted? – when one of the older members came rushing in saying, 'Jesus, Jesus Christ, haven't you guys heard?' He'd climbed up on a stool to change the channel on the old TV mounted high on the wall, changing it from the Golf Channel (a profile of Sergio Garcia, who'd recently won the Masters, how funny that Frank still remembered that) over to WRTV, the local station, out of Indianapolis. There was an aerial shot of a brown and white building, oddly familiar to Frank apart from the strobing blue lights of the police cars surrounding it, and a reporter's voice saying, 'Police have now closed off all roads and are evacuating residents in the vicinity as this remains very much a live shooter situation.' The yellow ticker tape at the bottom of the screen reading 'MANY FEARED DEAD IN SCHOOL SHOOTING IN SCHILLING, INDIANA ...' Frank started to hear a roaring noise in his ears.

'Oh Frank, oh Jesus,' one of them, Art or Ted, was saying, 'isn't that your wife's school?'

He didn't remember much immediately after that, though he must have got dressed and got in the car. The next thing Frank remembered was fighting with the cop, the guy manning the roadblock on Eisenhower, the street that led to the gates of Truman Elementary. 'MY WIFE AND KID ARE IN THERE!' Frank screamed at the guy.

'SIR! STAY BACK!'

You could hear it, in the distance, less than half a mile away – *pop pop pop pop pop pop*. Frank had launched himself at the officer, knocking him out of the way, trying to run. Then he was down on the asphalt himself, his ears ringing from the blow, another cop, who'd come from nowhere, standing over him, blocking out the sun, his nightstick in his hand, as he said, '*Don't make me arrest you, sir!*' Frank remembered the feeling of helplessness, of how, just a few years earlier, as editor of the *Gazette*, he could have got in there. If only there had been one of the older cops there, Chief Jacobs, someone like that. They knew Frank. They would have let him get closer. Closer so he could ... what?

Pop pop pop pop pop.

<u>*From the* Washington Post, *Saturday May 6, 2017*</u>

SCHILLING, INDIANA. A shooting rampage in this small Midwestern town on Friday afternoon left 22 people dead inside an elementary school, authorities said.

The dead included the suspected gunman, whom law enforcement sources have identified as Daniel Kemp, 21.

Police said that Kemp first apparently killed his father, Ted Kemp, at the home they shared in Schilling. Then he drove in his car to Truman Elementary.

In the car, authorities said, were three guns: a .223-caliber Bushmaster rifle and two pistols, a Sig Sauer and a Glock.

At the school Kemp proceeded to shoot and kill three adults – including the school's principal Michael Schneider – and 19 children. They were shot in two different rooms of the school, police said.

It has become the third deadliest school shooting in US history, after the massacres at Virginia Tech campus in Blacksburg, VA, and Sandy Hook in Connecticut. But the sheer scale of Friday's killing – and the nature of its victims, small children shot in the sanctuary of a school – deepened the horror, and unleashed a shaking kind of grief.

President Trump spoke about the shooting from the Oval Office, calling the shooter 'A coward. A loser,' before going on to say, 'The victims and their families are in our thoughts and prayers.' The president promised 'major, major action to prevent more tragedies like this,' but did not say specifically what he might do. 'I do want to thank the first responders,' Trump added. 'The police, the paramedics who were on the scene in, just record time, I think. Two or three minutes. Incredible when you think about it. Just record time.'

Among the dead were mother and son Pippa and Adam Brill, according to law enforcement sources. Pippa Brill had taught at the school for just over a year, when her five-year-old son Adam had been enrolled. 'Pippa was always enthusiastic, always smiling, always game to do anything,' said Chrissy Carson, a former president of the school's parent-teacher association.

In a phone interview, Carson choked up as she recalled Brill hugging students at the start of the school year. 'She was so loved by those kids.'

Joe Deering, who lived for a time on the same street as the Kemps, recalled Daniel Kemp as withdrawn, but not threatening in any way. 'I would just call him a socially awkward kid, I don't know, shy and quiet. Didn't look you in the eye,' Deering said in a telephone interview Friday night. 'Just kind of weird, maybe.'

Police described the school itself as one of the most horrific crime scenes they had ever encountered, and officials said the first-arriving responders would be given counseling. The gunman kept firing, keeping law enforcement officers at bay for nearly an hour after he fired the first shots. Tragically many of the victims may not have died right away.

Children who were evacuated from the school said later that they had been told to keep their eyes closed until they were outside. Police said that as the day went on they had accounted for every child who attended the school, tracking down even those who were absent because of illness.

The guns used in Friday's shootings were believed to have been purchased legally, and were registered to a family member of Daniel Kemp's, a law enforcement source said.

Police had been summoned by a number of 911 calls. Both state and local police converged on the school around 12.10 p.m. according to Indiana State Police Lt. L. Peter

Rance, and began 'a complete active shooter search of the building'.

In this small town south of Indianapolis, police cars began screaming toward the school. At First Trust bank, teller Jane Marcellus thought she saw 30 police cruisers. In the middle of a transaction one of her customers screamed, 'Oh my God! I have to get my kids!' Later, Marcellus learned she had a connection to the Kemp family: she had helped Ted Kemp with bookkeeping over the years, and had even bought a dog from him. Such connections are common in a small place like Schilling, she said. 'You can't get any closer to home than this. It's definitely going to affect this community badly.'

Police were finally able to enter the school at 1.48 p.m. and officers searched the classrooms for a shooter. When they found the gunman, however, he was dead by his own hand.

No officer fired a shot.

Frank often thought about the timings when he was doing the Computations: 1.05, when he first checked the time, just before that fellow ran in and turned the TV on. He'd taken, what? Two minutes to get dressed? Ten or fifteen to get down there? He'd been fighting with the cops by 1.25 at the latest. The shooting had gone on for at least another ten minutes while Frank sat screaming on the kerb. With every 'pop' of the *pop pop pop pop pop* Frank had the same thought: was that my wife? Was that my son? They found Pippa's body in a hallway. Kemp had shot her four times from behind with the 9mm Glock, at fairly close range, the bullets exiting approximately through her navel, mid-sternum, right breast (*the breast you saw for the first time in the milky light of that hotel bathroom*) and, with the last shot (Kemp clearly raking his fire upwards), the base of the skull. 'That last shot? It was a blessing, Frank,' Chief Jacobs told him a few days later. 'She'd have died instantly. Wouldn't know a thing about it from then on.' The skull shot exited out of her mouth, blowing teeth and tongue and gums all into a pulp. It felt like the strangest kind of blessing to Frank. But then, when he thought about what happened to his son, he guessed maybe it was. They found Adam in his classroom, the first one Kemp had entered. The ballistics reconstruction concluded that he'd sprayed the room with the Glock and the Sig Sauer, one pistol in each hand, emptying both weapons, firing twenty-five shots. He'd killed the teacher (Miss Janos) and six of the five-year-old students and wounded eight. Adam had been hit in the stomach as he tried to hide behind a bookcase. He'd bled to death sometime between being shot (approximately 12.31 – around the time, Frank later worked out, that he was hitting his drive on the eighteenth tee, a nice long draw that just cleared the bunker on the right, giving him a good line into the green) and the police entering the room at 1.48, a few minutes after Daniel Kemp put the gun in his own mouth. Oh the hours, countless, that Frank had put into reconstructing those seventy-seven minutes. Would his son have been calling out for his mother? For him? *'Please, Daddy! Help me, Daddy!'* How painful would it have been? Frank remembered accidentally trapping Adam's fingers in the kitchen door when he'd been three. He could still hear the screams. But this? Just trying to imagine it, even now, nearly a decade later, made him teeter back on his heels, reeling. Frank had been to enough shooting ranges in his time to know his son would have been smelling the cordite in the air, the sharp, acrid smell of gun smoke. He'd have been seeing and hearing his classmates crying out in pain. There were twenty-two kids in the class. Eight of them had not been hit. What had they been doing? Did they try to help each other? Did any of them comfort the ones who'd been shot? Frank tried to get in touch with the parents of a couple of survivors from Adam's class but was told they did not want to put their kids through the experience of reliving those moments.

So Frank was left, naturally, with his own imagination, which was happy to invent details for him: the puddles of blood on the floor, thick and oily, tiny fingers trying to hold in entrails, the exit wounds, big enough on adults, like saucers. On little kids? Like soup bowls, dinner plates. All the different little voices, high and shrill, crying 'Mummy! Mummy!', blending in a harmony from hell. The burn marks, the muzzle stamps, on the flesh of the ones shot at very close range. Incredibly, there was worse to come. Frank gave a brief interview to CNN a couple of days after the attack where, broken by grief, he mumbled something about the need to prevent these things from ever happening again. The clip went viral. Then he got the NRA people coming at him on social media, on Fox, calling him a communist. Calling him a queer. Calling him an actor. Some of them seized on the fact that his wife had been shot in the back, using it as proof that she'd been running away, that she'd been abandoning the children. (Frank knew exactly where Pippa had been running to –

Adam's classroom. She'd died in the hallway around twenty-five yards from it.)

'Fuck this fag and his coward bitch wife' @MAGASTEVE33
'Libtard Frank Brill sucks dicks' @patriothunter118822
'I bet this guy's kid died crying like a pussy' @trumper21

On and on it went. Frank kind of liked looking at this stuff. The shock of reading some of them was about the only thing that could punch through the numbness he was feeling in those months, back through the endless, miserable summer of 2017, when he started drinking again after three years sober, soon working his way through maybe a bottle and a half of vodka every day. Crying and wailing and shouting and gnashing his teeth as he wandered around the hot, empty house in his underwear. No more chilled Pinot Grigio to open when he heard her car in the driveway. No more carrot sticks.

Frank's grief would eventually be overshadowed by an even greater American tragedy, in the autumn of 2020, just before the election. In response to the Schilling school shooting President Trump had appointed a new gun tsar – the former NRA chairman Dale Beckerman. An odd choice, some felt. Beckerman came up with the policy the press came to call 'Rambo Teachers'. Gun-enthusiast educators were found in schools nationwide and given bonuses if they trained in armed combat and carried a weapon at all times during school hours. The policy was initially greeted with wild enthusiasm by the president's supporters. This waned even among the hardcore after the Coolidge High shooting in Kentucky. Two seventeen-year-old students, Lee Marks and Howard Devlin, entered the building armed with AR-15s and a range of handguns and proceeded to mow down their schoolmates. They were engaged by shop teacher Donald Lafferty (armed with his own AR-15) and the school's janitor, Walter Huff, who happened to keep a Beretta 9mm (as well as a fifth of Night Train) in his cleaning closet. Police estimated that over 3,000 rounds were expended in the resulting chaotic fire-fight. By the time the smoke cleared, ninety-four students and eight staff members (including Huff, shot in confusion by the police) were dead. A total of 102. Which now became the worst mass shooting in American history. Following Trump's re-election two months after the massacre Beckerman formulated and then passed the Coolidge Law: legalised open carry in every state in the USA.

Only one good thing had come out of this hellish time. The morning after the shooting at Adam and Pippa's school, the house phone had rung. Not unusual – it had been ringing every two minutes: the press, friends, cranks. Frank had let it go to voicemail, just lying there on the hall floor, drinking a beer, wondering where he was. Then he heard a girl's voice, high and shaky, saying, 'Hi, Dad. It's me. Olivia.'

Olivia, Frank's fifteen-year-old daughter.

The only child of his second marriage.

They hadn't spoken in two years.

FOUR

'That place is going to be the fifty-first state.'

A little after seven o'clock Frank printed off some maps and route plans, turned off the computer and headed out to eat. He hesitated at the car door, keys in hand. It was a two-minute drive or a ten-minute walk to Carlo's, his local diner. Having weighed up how cold it was against the need to get some exercise, he was just pocketing the car keys when he heard 'Evening, Frank', and turned to see old Mrs Rosen, his neighbour, coming along the sidewalk, walking her little dog.

'Oh. Hi, Rachel,' Frank said.

'Bitter cold,' Mrs Rosen said.

'Yeah. Had enough of it myself actually. I'm going to take off tomorrow. Head down to Florida for a few weeks. Play some golf.'

'Good for you, Frank. Quite right.'

Frank stamped his feet. 'Well, better get going.'

'You take care now, Frank. Enjoy the sunshine.'

'Sure will. Night, Rachel.'

She watched Frank head off beneath the bare branches of the avenue, shrugging down into his overcoat, seeking warmth, thinking what every neighbour who encountered Frank thought: you *poor, poor man*. Frank knew this. He didn't mind. He sang softly to himself – '*you take a little piece of me, with you ...*' – as he walked, breath pluming behind him in the dark night. At the top of his street he waited to cross Lincoln, the main road that ran west to east across the town. Frank had lived here his whole life. His parents, children and one of his three wives were all buried here. The air around him – thick with ghosts. But he didn't mind tonight. No, tonight Frank felt optimistic. Almost happy. Waiting for the lights to change he concentrated on his insides, trying to feel if it was really happening in there, this thing that was going to kill him. That had liberated him. That had finally made him green-light this thing he'd been thinking about for so long.

To his left, west, was downtown. To his right, east, was the area known as Barksdale. Little Germany they used to call it, where his high school, Jackson, had been. Thinking of this, a stray image flashed into his mind: him and his best friend Robbie McIntyre (orange file) in the spring of senior year, smoking a joint lying on the flat roof at the back of the school, overlooking the football field, where the team were training. You could hear the shouts of Coach Hauser in the distance, exhorting, pushing the jocks on. Robbie had been on the team. Then he wasn't. Frank recalled Robbie now, sitting up, red-eyed, drawing on the little one-skinner as he stared off into the sun and said to himself, '*That son-of-a-bitch* ...' That was all Robbie ever said about it. Should Frank have known then? Him and Robbie had been so close.

Then they graduated – Frank went to work at the paper and Robbie went off to college in North Carolina. The next time Frank saw Robbie was ten years later, at his funeral, laid out in a pine box, his skin so white. The first dead person Frank ever saw. Twenty-eight years old.

The lights changed and Frank crossed the street, communing with his dead in the cold Schilling night, the diner bright, the windows steamed up, Carlo moving around behind the grill in his whites, the waitresses in black with their coffee pots and water pitchers. The bell rang as he entered and a few people looked his way. Busy for a week night. He nodded a couple of 'hellos'.

That's poor Frank Brill.

His wife and son. His daughter too, you know.

Poor Frank.

Yeah, guess what, fuckos, Frank wanted to say. Now I've got the cancer too. How about that? Don't that beat all? 'Hey, Frank,' the young Mexican waitress he liked – Carmel? No, Carmen – was saying to him, already leading him to a booth. Young? She was probably in her late thirties. 'I saw you coming across the street,' she went on as she settled him in with menu and cutlery, pouring ice water. 'Cold night to be walking ...'

'Need the exercise.'

'No no. You in your prime. Diet Coke?'

'Please. What's the special?'

'Chicken pot pie.'

'That too. Thanks, Carmen.'

Frank took the file out of his jacket and laid it down beside his water glass. Laughter from the booth across from him, four guys, in their thirties, sharing a pitcher and chicken wings. He didn't know them. Looked like out-of-town. They all had their guns – three automatics, a big revolver – piled up on the table, barely enough room for the food and drink. You saw it all the time now. Folk would go to sit down for dinner and they'd have it digging into the small of their back, heavy under their armpit, even stuffed in their waistband (legally you were meant to have a holster, but this went pretty much unenforced in most states), so they all wound up on the table. The Coolidge Law. His drink arrived. Frank poured it into the frosted mug, not caring about the foam cresting over the rim, pooling on the table, and drummed his fingers on the orange file. File number one.

The List. How had it begun?

Three years ago, after Olivia. A psychologist would prob-ably have called it 'a coping strategy'. A way of directing his feelings of powerlessness and rage. But in recent months, since he'd started suspecting what had been confirmed in Dr Bowden's office earlier today, Frank had found himself applying himself to it with a new fervour. As the cancer had grown, so had The List. It had gone from two names, to three to four, until finally, and after much serious thought and calculation, to five.

Five names. A blend of the personal and the political, even though, with the political ones, it was still very personal.

Each of the names now had a file dedicated to them. Obviously some of these contained more research than the others, were demanding much more planning. But, yeah, as soon as the doctor had said the three magic words this afternoon, he'd known. Before Frank was even out of the place The List had gone from being any kind of psychological coping tool to being a real thing. In a way, he realised now, sipping his sugar-free soda, he'd been waiting for the diagnosis. Almost hoping for it. 'On a long enough timeline,' a doctor friend had told him once, 'everyone gets cancer.'

'And here you go, Frank. Need anything else?'

'I'm good, thanks.'

A big roar of laughter went up from the booth across. They'd had another pitcher delivered while Frank was waiting for his food. He cut into the crust of the pie and let the cloud of steam fill his face, mist his glasses. The filling — chunks of breast meat in thick chicken gravy studded with carrots and peas — was too hot to eat right away. Frank dunked a forkful of mashed potato in it and chewed. He could tell it was good, but of course he had no appetite, had been forcing himself to eat for a while. He ate slowly and reviewed his route plan, which formed a kind of appendix to the file. It'd changed a few times as he'd redrawn the order, finally deciding the chronology based on level of difficulty rather than geographical convenience. Walk before you could run and all that. It meant he'd be kind of criss-crossing the country a fair bit. But that was OK. Money didn't matter any more. He figured he had more than enough to see this through, or at least get as far as he was going to get with it. (Side note — he'd need to go to the bank tomorrow and withdraw a few thousand in cash, to cover travelling and accommodation expenses. He didn't want to be using credit cards any more than he had to, to avoid leaving any kind of paper trail.)

'It's an *investment*, man, for the next generation.'

'Bullshit. The place is uninhabitable, like forever, man.'

The guys across, louder as the fresh pitcher went down.

'Fuck you. There's people living in Hiroshima, right? In fucken *Hiroshima*. Am I right? How long did that take? Thirty or forty years?'

'Yeah,' another one of them entered the argument. 'Or that place in Russia. Cher-whatever. Years back. There's Russkis living there too now.'

'Yeah, but this, I mean, come on, guys. We fucken *destroyed* the place.'

'Fucken A.'

'I'm telling you. Thirty years. That place is going to be the fifty-first state. I'm telling you, man.'

They were talking about North Korea, about what was eventually going to happen to the 30,000-odd square miles that remained of it. In his last days in office Trump had been talking enthusiastically about the 'tremendous' construction opportunities the place offered. Frank kept his head down over his food.

'Golf courses, hotels, casinos ...'

'Hey, can we get the check please?'

'Like Vegas meets Hawaii, man.'

'Fucken A.'

'No, man, that's like over 15 per cent. Just leave a five. The bitch was slow. Food took like forever.' Frank listened to the guys stiffing Carmen on her tip.

The redevelopment of North Korea seemed to have become a lesser priority for President Ivanka. Indeed, in line with what many commentators on Fox were lamenting as the 'Trump-Lite' policies of new administration, the tone seemed to have softened, with less talk of 'to the victors the spoils' and more talk of the kind of stuff the international community was demanding: reparations for the surviving North Koreans, and all the South Koreans, and the northern Japanese, the people in Sapporo who'd been poisoned by the north-easterly winds that had prevailed in the aftermath of the surprise 200-megaton attack. Ivanka, it seemed, was more concerned with the optics of offending the world than her father had been, or indeed her brother was. Apparently it had been a close-run thing, whether Ivanka or Don Jr would be the one to succeed their father, to continue the dynasty. Don Jr played better with the base, the hardcore, but Ivanka had the potential to carry more teetering voters, more women, more, or at least some, of the college-educated. In the end they calculated – correctly – that the brand name would be enough to keep the base and Ivanka might even expand it slightly. (It was rumoured that even Trump himself had wondered if his son was not just too stupid, just too crazy.) But there were still difficult patches these days, when Ivanka talked too much of women's rights, or cosied up too much to the LGBT community. The base didn't like that shit. And Don Jr would get sent out on a hunting photo op in the Midwest. Or to scream abuse in an arena somewhere. There was talk now that they might pull a similar stunt again in the run-up to the 2028 election – dropping Hannity from the VP slot and installing Don Jr. See how it played out.

The gun guys were getting up to leave now. Frank looked at one of them, a beefy guy in check shirt and cargo pants, with a little goatee beard. He was slipping his weapon ostentatiously into a leather holster. Frank sighed and shook his head. The guy caught it. 'Excuse me?' he said.

'Huh?' Frank said.

'You got a problem, pal?

'The gun?' Frank nodded at the shoulder bulge.

The guy looked down at the check rubber grip of the automatic, almost like he was surprised to see it there, then back at Frank. 'Cocked and locked and on my hip 24/7, buddy ...'

'Real big man, huh?' Frank said quietly.

The guy's friends gathered around. Four of them standing over his booth, staring down. 'How's that, mister?' one of the others said.

'Big men. Throwing your guns around, scaring people.'

The goatee guy stepped towards Frank. One of the others put a hand on his arm. 'Just leave this fuck, Al,' he said.

'You don't carry like a good American?' Goatee said.

'TRUMP!' the other guy yelled in his face. 'TRUMP! You don't like it – get the fuck out.'

TRUMP! TRUMP! You still heard it all the time now, in the street, in bars, arguments. It didn't matter that he'd been out of office for more than two years. It served as a simple declaration of all they believed in. A one-word credo. The brand.

'Hey! Please! That's enough!' Carmen said, appearing, Carlo behind her. 'There's families trying to eat here.'

'Fuck you, bitch! You got papers? Huh? Papers?'

'Maybe we'll call ICE on your beaner ass.'

'Out. Get out.' This was Carlo.

'There goes your tip, bitch.'

'Just leave.'

They shouldered past them, heading for the door as the other diners kept their heads down over their food, not making eye contact. 'TRUMP, BITCHES!' Goatee yelled as he left, getting a supportive 'TRUMP!' back from one stray customer. The bell clanged and it was quiet again.

'Frank,' Carlo said. 'You shouldn't make so much trouble.'

FIVE

'The quickest route is the one you know ...'

The next morning, a Saturday, and Frank was up early as usual, before the sun. He packed briskly and efficiently. One large wheelie suitcase with enough clothes and toiletries for about a week. (He'd be needing clothes for longer than that, but he figured he could just buy new ones on the way and discard the old stuff.) He filled a suit bag with his good dark blue suit – the one Olivia had helped him pick out for Pippa and Adam's funeral, the only time he'd worn it – a sport coat and a couple of ties, because who knows? He might go somewhere nice. A last meal, something like that. Into his shoulder bag went the laptop, chargers, the five files, spare legal pads, his .22 Woodsman and a box of ammunition. He knew the Woodsman would never be enough for all of this, but he figured it'd work for #1 and then he'd review from there. He packed his luggage into the trunk and went back inside.

At the kitchen table, over coffee, light just beginning to soften the darkness outside, Frank reviewed his route: out of town and then south until he picked up the I-64 which he'd take west to St Louis. Bit of luck and he'd be there by lunchtime. A quick bite and then take the I-44 south for about eight hours, all the way to Oklahoma City.

It wasn't much more than twelve hours straight driving but it felt like all this time the guy had been living in another country, on another planet.

Frank filled his flask with the rest of the coffee from the pot and turned all the appliances off. He turned the heating off. He made sure the back door was locked. He propped the letter up on the mantelpiece, where it was sure to be found, stood in the hallway and took a last look around. He felt like he should be feeling something more, knowing he would never be returning. That this should feel like something worth commenting on. But all he could think to say was what Adam used to say whenever they went away on vacation, down to the house in Florida. 'Bye-bye, House,' Adam used to say.

'Bye-bye, house,' Frank said.

Frank picked up breakfast at McDonald's, a sausage-egg McMuffin and a hash brown – why worry about the cholesterol and the weight gain now? It was about the only thing he liked from McDonald's, but he found he could only take a couple of bites. He was at the bank just after it opened, where there was already a line. He nodded hellos to a few folks while he waited. (*Poor Frank. That poor man.*) Having been the editor, coupled with his tragic personal history, meant a lot of people in Schilling knew Frank better than he knew them. Which was one of the reasons he rarely went out any more, least of all downtown on a Saturday morning, but he couldn't get more than a few hundred bucks from the ATM so he hadn't much choice. Ah shit, here was some guy now, some old fella Frank recognised from the golf club, on his way over, tucking a deposit slip into the back pocket of his Farah slacks. 'Hey, Frank,' the guy said. 'How ya doing?'

'Good, good ...'

'Always a line, right?'

'Always.' There was only one bank now. Used to be lots.

'Not seen you up at the club much lately?'

'My knee. Shot to hell. Might have to get a new one.'

'Aw darn.'

'Yep.'

'What can you do, Frank? You get old.'

'That's right.'

'I was just saying to Freddie Lewis the other day, you remember Freddie? He –'

The light went up saying the next teller was free. 'Damn, sorry, I got to –'

'No problem. Don't let me keep you. Take it easy.'

'Sure. Bye.'

Frank handed over his withdrawal slip. The teller frowned. She was young, pretty, about the same age as his daughter was. Would have been. 'I'm sorry, Mr Brill, but this is for three thousand dollars.'

'So? There's got to be fifteen thousand in that account.'

'Yes, but we really need prior notification for cash withdrawals over two thousand dollars.'

'Since when?'

'Oh, a few years now. We just don't carry as much cash as we used to. People these days tend to –'

Frank sighed and leaned on the counter. 'Can you help me out here?'

'Ah, just a minute …'

She hurried off. *People these days tend to* … Yeah, Frank thought, they tend to pay for a goddamn can of soda or a candy bar with a credit card. Contactless this, Apple Pay that. Saw a kid the other week trying to buy a banana from a market stall with his phone. Swear to God. Fella was pissed when it wouldn't fly too. Probably soon enough it would. Cash would be gone. There would be upsides – they'd get rid of that new hundred-dollar bill, the one with Trump on it, his face sketched lean, his shoulders muscular as he stared proudly into the mid-distance. One of the first things Ivanka did. Apparently folk in California were refusing to use them. Yeah, a kid trying to buy a banana with a phone. That was where we were now. *Jesus, listen to yourself*, he thought. *You sound like an old man*. Still, maybe best not make too much of a fuss, draw attention to himself. He could always go the ATM and top up whatever she gave him. Here she was now, bustling back, smiling. Frank looked over to the office door she had come from and saw the manager, Ben what's-his-name, looking over this way. He'd been a few years below Frank in school. 'That's all fine, Mr Brill, sorry for the hold-up. Now, how would you like the cash?'

With twenty hundred-dollar bills, Trump's face staring up at him, ten fifties, twenty twenties and ten tens in an envelope tucked in his inside pocket, Frank was gassed up, back behind the wheel and heading west out of town by

9.25 a.m., an FM station he liked on the radio and the heat set just right.

He joined the 64 at Carefree (ha!), about fifteen miles north of where the Ohio River formed the border with Kentucky, made a right onto the freeway and was soon rolling through Hoosier National Forest, bare sycamore trees stretching away on either side of the highway as he headed west with the rising sun at his back. He'd never been through here in winter before. For Frank, Hoosier Forest would always mean summer holidays in the early, happy days of his first marriage, back in the late eighties and early nineties, back when they didn't have so much money. As often happened when you were driving long distances alone, Frank's mind slipped into the past as the tarmac sizzled beneath his wheels ...

Grace's parents – old Tony Deefenbach and his wife Marge – had owned a cabin near Lake Monroe. Two bedrooms and five acres of woods. There had been a little pond, a fire pit with a grill. Frank still in his early twenties. He could drink back then, like you could when you were younger. Him and Tony sitting out on the porch after dinner while the girls did the dishes (man, you try that shit now, Frank thought), knocking back, what was that stuff old man Deefenbach used to drink? Amaretto. Sweet tooth. Like a lot of those old-timers who grew up in the Depression. Tough old guy though. Big. Shaved head. Huge Reagan fan. Was at Normandy. It was Tony who gave him the Woodsman and taught him how to use it, out in the trees behind the cabin, popping and plinking away at bottles and cans ('Darn it, Frankie, squeeze it now! Like a tit!'), the .22 cartridges small and slippery as Tic-Tacs in Frank's clumsy hands as he tried to reload the magazine, dropping them onto the leaves and pine needles, pissing the old boy off. He hadn't been a bad man, Tony.

And he'd liked Frank, Frank who had broken his heart, going and cheating on his daughter like that, going off with Cheryl, right after Grace had that miscarriage too. They'd never spoken again after that night, him and Tony, after ... now when exactly would it have been? He'd taken Cheryl to see *Titanic*, one of their first proper dates after all the sneaking around, and got home to a ringing phone. 1997. The old guy in his late seventies by then, drunk and ugly and mean as he said, '*You son-of-a-bitch, you no-good cheating son-of-a-bitch,*' and all Frank could say was 'I'm sorry, Tony. I didn't mean to hurt her. I'm sorry.' Cheryl coming out of the bathroom and Frank hanging up and saying, 'Wrong number.' And then it all got worse when Grace went off and married that asshole dentist who took all her money. And a lot of Tony's money too, as a matter of fact. It wasn't Frank's fault she'd married him, of course. She'd been angry and hurt and on the rebound and in her mid-thirties with no kids or anything and maybe thinking she'd be left on the shelf and all that. But then, if Frank hadn't left her for Cheryl maybe it would all have been different and Grace wouldn't have wound up becoming a drunk. (The Computations: *If X hadn't happened then Y wouldn't have happened and then ...*) Old man Deefenbach had died a few years later. Frank not welcome at the funeral. Yeah, he'd done some terrible things. Caused more than his fair share of pain and upset. But there was a chance, rolling towards him now on the bright morning macadam, that he could still put a few of them right.

His phone chirruped, Waze telling him that there was a faster route available, but Frank ignored it, deciding he'd stick with the 64. It reminded him of a conversation he'd had with Tony, funnily enough, who'd once said to him, way back, long before Wayz and Google Maps and GPS and all this stuff, when Frank was dropping Grace off after one of their first dates and wondering what was the best route to take to get back to his parents' place. 'You know, son,' Tony said, putting his hand on Frank's shoulder there in the hall, Grace and her mom just visible in the kitchen behind him, the clatter of pots and pans being put away, the aroma of some dinner still clinging to the air (chicken, paprika), 'the quickest route is always the one you know.'

Frank had surely had many more important conversations in his life than that one. The one where he broke up with Grace for a start. Why should that one still be stuck in his mind now, an entire generation later? Why could he recall a specific phrase from it and exactly where he was standing when it was uttered when he couldn't recall a single line from any one of a hundred undoubtedly more major conversations?

Ach, the things you remembered.

Frank was brought back into the world by the sound of his tyres sizzling over metal and he realised he was on a bridge, crossing the Wabash River, the western dividing line between Indiana and Illinois.

Out in the wildlands now, the long, barren stretches beside the Wabash, the tri-state area that encompassed north-west Kentucky, south-west Indiana and south-east Illinois. He realised over an hour must have passed from the forest. He yawned, the muscles in his jaw cricking. Bad sign that, only snapping out of it with the sound of the surface changing beneath his wheels. He saw a sign for a Road King a few miles over the bridge. Coffee. Snack. Top up the tank. Rest the old eyeballs for a minute or two. 'Can we stop, Dad? Please can we?' his kids used to say. Then the 'YAYYY!' when he said yes. His dead kids.

* * *

Frank pulled into the lot, finding a space right in front, parking under the red-white-and-blue signage. He hadn't been at a Road King in a while, a lot more of them in Illinois than over in Indiana. They'd substantially changed their logo over the last decade. It had always had red-white-and-blue elements but now it was more so: pretty much a giant Stars and Stripes. A 'Support Our Troops' below it that looked pretty much permanent too.

He cranked his seat back and rested his eyes for a moment, lowering the window down a couple of inches to let some cold air in, the sounds of the lot drifting in too – the big trucks hissing and squealing as they stopped and started, the *dingdingding* of people trying to get their pumps going, the hum and clank of the electronic doors as customers came and went, the blasts of horns from the highway, snatches of music – rock, hip hop, pop – coming from the opening and closing car doors, fragments of conversations, in English, in Spanish (something you didn't hear too much these days, people tended to keep that to themselves), the cries of children, all the sounds of American travel carrying on the breeze.

Inside the store, bright and loud, Frank paid a long, complex visit to the can (he would spare us the details here) and picked up some mints and a styrofoam beaker of coffee. Joining the line to pay, he tuned in and out of the muzak – an instrumental version of 'Livin' La Vida Loca' – and the conversations floating around him – '*I told you "no", young lady … when we get there … Did you get me sugar in this? … I'm just gonna use the restroom … I'll meet you back at the car … Oh, grab me some peanut brittle …*' He gazed at the windows and shelves with tired eyes, automatically sub-editing the handwritten signage dotted around the store: a mortuary of redundant or missing apostrophes and grammatical howlers, things like 'tea' and 'coffee' with their inverted commas of wild promise and the spelling of the madman loosed everywhere – '*Lifes to short too drink cheap beer*' one sign said. The editor inside Frank still raged at all of this and wondered if the downfall of America wasn't somehow connected to it. But he was too old and too tired to put it together into a coherent theory. Besides, someone had probably already done so. In the *Atlantic*. In the *New Yorker*. Someone younger and cleverer than him.

It was funny. A decade ago, way back in 2016, the state he was now standing in, Illinois, had returned Clinton with damn near 60 per cent of the vote (Chicago swaying the thing of course), while just a few miles away, back across the Wabash where he'd come from, Indiana had gone for Trump by the same margin. Not so much any more: Ivanka still lost Illinois in 2024, but by a much narrower margin. And it didn't matter, by then the electoral map of the country looked like a blood smear squashed under a micro- scope slide, a red gobbet with a few flecks of blue virus in it – California, New York. Frank wondered how it would look two years down the line, in '28.

Well, he wouldn't be around to see that.

All at once there was the sound of squealing rubber and the necks of everyone in the line jerked to the right to see two black vans come roaring into the gas station. Before they had even stopped men were jumping out and running towards the store, all of them wearing flak jackets and helmets, carrying rifles and clubs. Mayhem broke out in the line up front as two guys – Mexicans – started to run for the back of the store, one knocking over a display of dips, jars of salsa smashing on the tiled floor. One of the Mexicans went barrelling through a door marked 'EMPLOYEES ONLY'. The other one tried to follow but was football-tackled by a big biker just as the squad burst in the front. 'That's not necessary, sir, we have this!' one of them shouted at the biker, who was punching the struggling Mexican on the ground.

'Don't be alarmed, folks!' another helmeted guy shouted. 'Just stand back please!'

Frank saw it now, on the backs of their flak jackets: ICE.

There was shouting and screaming from out on the forecourt: more officers were surrounding a pickup truck, forcing a family out at gunpoint. A couple of families it looked like: two Mexican women, several small children, all crying. The guy who'd burst out the back door suddenly reappeared too – being frogmarched around the side of the building by two more ICE officers who'd clearly been waiting. He was shouting something to his family over and over – '*No te preocupes! Papá regresará en un rato! No te preocupes! Papá regresará en un rato!'* — as they pushed him towards the van. On the floor, just ten yards away from where Frank stood, clutching his shopping to him, they were finishing up cuffing the other guy, hauling him to his feet. A few people were shouting at the officers — 'Hey! Easy now! Let him be!' — but more were shouting at the Mexican guy and congratulating the biker. A woman about Frank's age was filming the whole thing on her phone and an ICE officer snatched it from her. 'HEY!' she shouted. 'You can't do that!' But he could, of course. The Extreme Patriot Act, in 2022, after the bombing in San Francisco, part of the measures making it illegal to *'interfere with government officials performing their duties in any way, including unauthorized filming or sound recording'*. As the Mexican guy was led out past Frank, bleeding, a man shouted after him: 'WON'T BE NO MORE OF THIS WHEN WE GET THE WALL FINISHED!' This got a few whoops and cheers. Frank watched as the women and children were loaded into one van, the two men into another, and, with sirens and lights, the vans disappeared back onto the highway. Chatter resumed among the people in the line. The biker took another high five. The musak became audible once again, 'Livin' La Vida Loca' fading out now, the whole thing having taken less time than the three or four minutes of the song.

An employee was already on her hands and knees sweeping up broken glass and salsa. Outside two ICE officers were talking to the woman whose phone they'd taken, filling in a form and handing her a receipt, telling her she'd get it back in 'four to six weeks'. The officers walked off towards their car. 'What about due process?' the woman shouted after them. 'Hey, bitch!' the biker shouted. 'They was *due* and they got *processed*!' This got a few laughs. Frank turned, shaking his head, and caught the eye of a girl behind him in the line. 'Fast, ain't they?' she said. 'Happens a lot at interstate gas stations these days. They got that new license-plate recognition wired right into Homeland Security.' Frank looked at her. She smiled, leaned in conspiratorially and said, 'My boyfriend's a state trooper.'

SIX

'What did you end up doing with your life?'

Frank's head jerked up from the pillow as headlights raked his room, snapping him out of a bad dream and into the tumbling confusion felt by someone towards the end of their life waking up in an unfamiliar location. In this case Belmont Suites, off the 44, on the western outskirts of Oklahoma City. He picked up his phone – 6.53 a.m. Still dark out. He turned on the bedside lamp and took in the room he'd fallen asleep in, fully clothed, around 10.30 the night before. Two double beds, TV set, fridge, armchair and a little hallway leading to the bathroom. $49.95 a night including complimentary breakfast buffet. He could have afforded a better place, but the Belmont had fulfilled his one major criterion: it accepted cash payments, no credit card required so long as you didn't need your phone activated. Which he didn't. Frank sat up and swung his legs out of bed. A trait common to the ex-drinker – he loved mornings. Every night when he climbed between the sheets he savoured a feeling familiar to any alcoholic: I made it. I made it through another whole day. I am getting into bed completely sober. This feeling had its morning corollary: a minor flicker of panic, of terror, in that moment of waking, the moment between sleep and true wakefulness, when a hangover is automatically anticipated. Then the flooding joy of pure relief when he realised he did not have one, that the routine experience of almost thirty years has not been repeated, that you have slept deeply for six or seven hours (no multiple trips to the bathroom, no night terrors, no constant waking) and that you will be getting out of bed and into the day clear, fresh and unimpeded.

He stripped off, throwing his dirty clothes into the corner, and took a long, hot shower. After the shower he dressed – check shirt, jeans, sweater – and wandered along to reception where he helped himself to his 'complimentary breakfast', well, a styrofoam cup of coffee, choosing to ignore the baskets of stale pastries and 'power bars' that constituted the rest of it. He went back to his room and shaved for the first time in three or four days, taking his time, steaming coffee cup at his elbow, finding himself whistling a tune, for all the world like a regular man getting ready for the day, going to a job, with a wife and kids somewhere off in the house, like the man he was a long time ago. (Of course, he never completely stopped thinking about the cancer, up in there, burrowing away around the upper reaches of his colon, looking to spread, to enlarge its kingdom, looking for metastasis.) Funny how all the crap they told you when you were a kid turned out to be true – '*sleep on it ... it'll all look better in the morning ... it's a wonder what a good night's rest can do ...*' While he shaved he glanced now and then at the orange file open on the counter beside the sink, at the photographs, printed off Google Street Maps. 'Doxxing' they called it. The word hadn't existed back in the eighties, when Frank started out as a reporter, but it pretty much meant doing what you did back then. Tracking people down. Much easier these days though ...

Starting off with the newspaper stories that ran when the scandal broke, and going by what he'd heard over the years from local rumour and innuendo, Frank had moved on to Facebook, where a thorough trawl through the public page of one of the guy's relatives had yielded a good few clues as to location (the bulky figure, much aged but clearly recognisable, lurking in the background of a few photo-graphs – Thanksgivings, birthday parties) before hitting the Oklahoma state voter rolls and finally coming up with the address.

Going against the rush-hour traffic, everyone else heading into the city, with a country station on the radio, Frank found the suburb in a little over fifteen minutes. He parked the car a couple of hundred yards along from the address and watched the street. Two cars left their driveways, hurried-looking men, late for work. A UPS van cruised down; the guy went up to a door with a parcel, got his signature on the little screen and left. Then nothing. Frank was aware that his heart rate was high, his fingers alive with electric current, his mouth dry.

Was he really about to do this? Frank, who had never even been in a bar fight in his life. Yes. Yes, he was. He wanted answers. He wanted to hear that ancient, rusty forgotten thing – the truth.

He pulled his leather gloves on as he crossed the street. Then up the steps and onto the wooden porch, glancing left and right. No one around. The sound of the doorbell, a weak digital tune, Frank looking up and down the street again, still nothing, all the houses similar to this one, detached bungalows in pastel colours with porches and small front lawns. He hit the bell again and now a voice from inside, an old man's voice, low and gruff, saying 'Hold on!', heavy footsteps. The door opened. A tall man in sweatpants and a vest stood there: in his mid-seventies, thinning grey hair, stooped now, but still a dominating presence. 'Yeah?' he said.

'Hi,' Frank said. 'Remember me?'

The guy squinted at him.

'Frank Brill, coach.'

The use of 'coach' registered. 'What the fuck do you want?' Hauser said.

Frank took his hand out of the pocket of his overcoat, the .22 in his fist. He levelled it at Hauser's belly. 'I want to talk.' When Frank had played this scene out in his mind he'd sounded suave, impossibly cool. Like Clint Eastwood or Mel Gibson. Now, standing here, he heard his own voice shrill, dry and high in his eardrums. He'd also been counting on more fear from Hauser as soon as he produced the gun. But the former coach was just standing there, looking confused and angry.

'What the fuck is this?' Hauser was saying now.

'Back in the house,' Frank said, gesturing with the gun, having to concentrate hard to keep the barrel from shaking as he stepped forward. 'Put your hands up.' Hauser took a couple of steps back and raised his hands, palms up at chest height, like someone reluctantly playing cops and robbers with a kid. Frank stepped inside and shut the door behind him. What now? 'Right . . .' Frank said. 'OK. Sit . . . sit down.'

Hauser sighed as he lowered himself into a hardback chair against the wall. Frank wanted to sit down too, his legs were rippling and trembling. Hauser was watching him intently, the hard, cruel grey eyes Frank remembered from gym class not leaving him. 'You OK, son?' Hauser asked.

'Shut up, Hauser,' Frank said. Now that felt good. How many times had he wanted to say that back in the day? But Hauser just laughed.

'OK,' he said.

'What's so funny?' Frank asked.

'You,' Hauser said. 'Brill. I remember you. Class of '84. Fucking weed. Couldn't even throw a ball. Good for nothing. What did you end up doing with your life?'

This wasn't how Frank saw it going. He was the one with the gun here. He'd be asking the questions. 'Shut up!' Frank said. 'I'm asking the fucking questions here!'

'What do you want to know?' Hauser said calmly.

No, Frank hadn't seen it going this way at all. He lowered himself slowly into a club chair opposite Hauser, keeping the gun on him. 'Robbie McIntyre,' Frank said finally.

From the Greensboro Sentinel, *June 18, 1993*

A man found dead in his home on Scarsdale Road, Greensboro, last week has been identified as Robert McIntyre, 28. Mr McIntyre was found by a neighbour on Friday after fumes began to escape from his garage. Police confirmed that they are not looking for anyone else in connection with the death.

From the Schilling Gazette, *March 17, 2010*

Jackson High School has announced the resignation of Coach Martin Hauser, amid claims that he sexually molested several boys in the 1970s and 80s. Hauser, who had been due to retire later this year, has strenuously denied the allegations. In a statement released Monday, Principal Katherine Saunders said: 'I can confirm that Martin Hauser is no longer employed by the school. We will be making no further comment at the present time.' Hauser was first accused of sexual assault in a Facebook posting by former Jackson High student Jason Farr in December last year. Several other students have since come forward to corroborate Farr's claims. Schilling Police have confirmed that they have interviewed Hauser and are investigating the allegations. Interviewed by the *Gazette* yesterday outside his home, former Coach Hauser said: 'I continue to deny these wild, unsubstantiated claims.'

'You raped him,' Frank said. 'You raped him when he was seventeen years old.'

Hauser laughed and shook his head. 'No I didn't. Another one of those damn kids with a stupid grudge because they didn't get picked for the team one week.'

'Bullshit.'

'Jury didn't think so. Found me innocent.'

'I want to know the truth.'

'Or what?'

'What?'

'What are you going to do, Brill? Shoot me? Look at you. You're shaking like a leaf. Never shot anything in your damn life.'

'Listen. I'm not kidding here.'

'Yeah, I think we're done.' Hauser started to get up.

'Sit down!' Frank said.

'Just get out of here before I call –'

'SIT DOWN!' Frank yelled, rising.

'– the cops and –'

BANG!

Frank shot Hauser in the right thigh.

'AH! MOTHERFUCKER!' Hauser screamed, going down, clutching his leg. 'MOTHERFUCKER!'

'You see!' Frank said. 'Now tell me the truth!'

Hauser looked up at Frank, his eyes glittering with pain and rage. No, he really hadn't thought Frank would shoot him.

'Ahhhgh. You fucking maniac!' Hauser said. 'You know what you're doing? You're going to kill an innocent man over some bullshit lies from over forty years ago?'

'Robbie killed himself, Hauser. Did you know that?'

'What's that got to do with me? I AIN'T NO DAMN PAEDOPHILE! Fuck! FUCK!' Blood was spreading across

Hauser's grey sweatpants, soaking between his fingers, dripping onto the hardwood floor. Frank felt sick. He stepped backwards, fighting nausea. He looked around the room. There, on the table, was a laptop. Something occurred to Frank. He took a deep breath, steadying himself, then walked over and opened it. 'What's the password?'

Now, for the first time, a flicker of fear crossed Hauser's face. But he got it under control. 'Go fuck yourself,' he said. Frank shot at his other leg, missed, hit the floor, pulled the trigger again and hit him in the left shin. Hauser *screamed*. 'Ahhh ... motherfucker, *motherfucker!*'

'The password!' Frank repeated. Hauser was sweating and bleeding heavily now. He looked up at Frank, defiance still burning in his eyes. Frank aimed the gun at his foot. Hauser held his hand up. 'No! Wait! Wait ... endgame52. All lower case.' Frank typed it in and got Hauser's home screen. He went straight to last night's search history.

There it all was.

Hundreds of images, some of them tough to look at. Really young boys. Some pre-teen.

'OK. Listen –' Hauser said.

Frank levelled the gun at his chest, closed his eyes and pulled the trigger five times – *POPPOPOPPOPPOP.*

The sound of the spent brass cartridges tinkling onto the hardwood floor. The soft thunk of a couple of stray shots going into the wall or the floor beside Hauser's head. Frank opened his eyes and saw Hauser was slumped on his side, a huge pool of blood spreading out from under him.

Frank just made it to the wastepaper basket in the corner before he doubled over and threw up – a hot broth of coffee and stomach acid. He sat there for a long time, shaking, his heart rate gradually climbing down.

In the kitchen he ran cold water over his wrists and face, rinsed his mouth out and dried himself with a paper towel. The kitchen was small, well kept, and smelled of lemon disinfectant. There were family photos on the fridge – nieces and nephews maybe. He wandered through the bungalow, the smell of cordite in every room now. In the laundry room he found a trash can full of empty vodka bottles, a cheap supermarket brand. In a suitcase under the bed in the main bedroom he found a raft of magazines, a softer, more commercial version of the kind of images on the laptop. In the closet there was a big dresser. Rooting through the top drawer – socks, underwear, ties and cufflinks – he felt a metal bump and pulled out a pistol, a Glock, absurdly heavy in his fist after the Woodsman. He ejected the magazine – the 9mm slugs looking fat and swollen compared to the .22s. Frank popped the mag back in, made sure the safety was on and tucked the pistol into the back of his jeans.

In the next drawer down he found a photo album, the kind common back before everyone had a whole library of photos on their phone. He flipped through a few pages, family celebrations, and whatnot. Some badly taken snaps of the coach receiving awards at various receptions. Lots of photos of him with the various football teams he'd coached in his career. Frank turned another page and stopped. There on the field out back of the school was Coach Hauser with Robbie, Robbie still in football uniform, still on the team. Hauser had his arm around him. Both of them grinning. With gloved hand, Frank took the photo out from underneath the thin sheet of clear plastic and turned it over. On the back, handwritten, it just said *'Robbie M, Sept 1982'*. Frank looked at the photograph for a long time. Then he dropped it back on top of the album, left it on top of the dresser and walked out of the bedroom.

He went down the hall, through the living room, side-stepping the spreading puddle of blood, and out the front door, not looking at the body of Coach Hauser at all.

SEVEN

'We serve our sides family-style.'

The murderer Frank Brill kept his hands clamped on the steering wheel, trying to keep them from shaking, trying to keep the damn car on the road.

Oklahoma to Phoenix was pretty much a straight shot west on the 40, about sixteen hours, dipping down into northern Texas, through New Mexico and Arizona. Frank's plan had him stopping for the night about halfway, around Albuquerque.

It had given him no pleasure. He'd been reminded of how he'd felt when his pop took him fishing the first time and he'd had to kill a trout. How much it had wriggled and fought for life. How bright its blood was on its gills, on its milky underbelly. The sickening feeling as Dad brought the squat, wooden baton down on its skull. No, it hadn't been any kind of fun back in that house. He remembered *The Sopranos* guy – Gandolfini was it? He died. Heart attack, in Europe somewhere – playing a hit man in that film, more than thirty years back now – '*The first time you kill somebody, that's the hardest. I don't give a shit if you're fuckin' Wyatt Earp or Jack the Ripper. First one is tough, no fuckin' foolin'. That's the bitch of the bunch. The second one … the second one ain't no fuckin' Mardis Gras either, but it's better than the first one … it's more diluted, it's … it's better. Then the third one … the third one is easy. It's no problem. Now … shit … now I do it just to watch their fuckin' expression change.*' Well, Frank wasn't ever going to get to there. But he hoped it would get easier. After a couple of hours, coming up on Amarillo, he noticed he was still shaking. It had been so long since he'd felt it that it took him a few seconds to properly place the sensation.

Hunger.

He realised he hadn't eaten a single thing since his attempted breakfast, more than twenty-four hours ago.

The restaurant was called Rusty's Steakhouse. A big wood-framed building, plenty of cars out front and rock 'n' roll music on the in-house sound system as a check-shirted waitress led Frank to a booth and settled him with a menu and ice water. The place was busy. Across from Frank a family of four came in. Mom and Dad had to be weighing in at close to three hundred pounds apiece, their two teenage boys not far behind on the scales. 'Don't give us no booth,' the man was saying to the waitress, 'we can't fit in no booth.' Frank scanned the menu: baby back ribs, fried dill pickles, mountain oysters, onion rings. The insane edifices of the sandwiches – char-broiled chicken, pulled pork, beef, buffalo – and then the steaks: centre cuts, panhandle, Dallas cut, Fort Worth cut, Texan strips, going all the way up to seventy-two ounces, four and a half pounds of meat, which came free if you finished it. Frank ordered the ten-ounce sirloin – about the smallest cut they had – medium rare with fries and grilled mushrooms. All for $17.95. Probably the equivalent of a handful of arugula and a green juice in this joint. 'Anything to drink there, hon?' the waitress asked.

'Just a Diet Coke, thanks.'

'Coming right up.'

At another table there was a group of four young women, all in their early twenties, all with babies. There were a lot of babies in the restaurant in general, Frank now becoming aware of a certain background level of crying and wailing. It figured – Texas was one of the first states to go for the ban, four or five years back, when it was optional for a short time, before it became law, mandatory everywhere. Frank looked at the babies, wondering what it might have been like to be a grandfather.

Olivia hadn't told him anything about it, even though she and Frank were back on good terms again, having gradually rebuilt their relationship in the years after she'd rung him, the morning after the madman had killed Frank's wife and son. They'd not spoken for a couple of years, after her mom, Cheryl, Frank's second wife, had sat her down and told her the real reason her marriage to Frank had broken down when she was six.

Frank's daughter had been brought up with the traditional fictions of divorce – *we grew apart ... Mommy and Daddy loved each other very much, but we couldn't live together ... we're just very different people ... we'll both always love you ...* and so on and so forth. Well, just after Olivia turned fourteen, Cheryl took her out to dinner, got the best part of a bottle of Chardonnay inside her, and told Olivia that all that stuff was a bunch of bullshit and the real reason they split up was that she found a load of texts on his phone and figured out that he'd been banging some girl called Pippa, some piece much younger than her. She'd thrown Frank out the house and that was that and she wasn't a little kid any more and why should she be the one who had to lie to cover for Frank's adulterous ass when she'd never done anything wrong? Fuck him and, well, you know the truth now.

Frank got the call a couple of nights later.

You bastard, Dad. How could you do that to Mom? All these years telling me this bullshit. I never want to speak to you again. And Frank just saying the only thing he could – *I'm sorry. I'm so sorry.* Over and over again.

It would take the death of her stepmom and half-brother for her to speak to her father again. And, once they had, Frank responded like a man. Which is to say he took her out to dinner and got very drunk and broke down crying and asked for her forgiveness. Which the sixteen-year-old Olivia, once again his only child, gave him.

In the years that followed they'd grown close once again. She went off to college in Indianapolis and Frank would drive up sometimes and take her out to eat. Slip her a little extra money. He thought of the last time he saw her, just before Christmas, three years ago. They'd gone to an Italian restaurant she liked, near the college. Living on her own for the first time, Olivia said, had made her grow up a lot. She realised how difficult life was. How many choices you had to make. Frank had looked at his daughter – twenty-two years old now, in her senior year, sat across from him, drinking legally and everything, and she still looked like the little girl who'd sit in his lap at the dinner table and he'd sneak her a weak spritzer, just a splash of white wine topped up with soda water, and hope she wouldn't have problems with drinking as she got older, like he did, and, oh God, the pain he'd caused her in her young life but maybe it would all still be all right.

It wasn't.

They'd had to piece it all together after she died, from her friends, her room-mate, the police. They never found out who the guy was. It hadn't been anyone she'd been seeing seriously. Her friends knew that. It had been a party, a one-night thing. Then she'd found out she was pregnant. Indiana had always been tough. Way back in 2016, Pence, governor at the time, had signed a bill trying to prohibit women from getting an abortion due to diagnosis of disability. The bill also proposed that the identities of abortion providers be made public, that funerals be held for fetal remains and that women undergo an ultrasound at least eighteen hours prior to undergoing the procedure. (Of course, this was all long before whatever happened with Pence in that DC hotel suite. No one would ever really know for sure. Pence resigned and denied everything, but rumours abounded on the left and right: he was set up by the Clintons, he was set up by Trump to make way for Ivanka, he was slathered in amyl nitrate and sucking off a black kid. Nothing happened. Everything happened. As ever, in all the churn, no one ever knew what really went on. *'Mike Pence had very little to do with my policies or my election!'* Trump had tweeted at the time.) Anyway, in 2017, after Pence had gone to the White House, the new governor,

Holcomb, had signed a law that required abortion providers to report detailed patient information to the state. His supporters said the law would ensure safe abortions, but, in reality, it helped stigmatise the procedure. The ACLU fought the case and lost. Anti-abortion groups celebrated. 'A BIG weekend for LIFE in Indiana!' All that stuff. But this was nothing, just a prelude to the big one.

Overturning Roe v Wade.

It had been the biggest triumph of Trump's second term, when the Republicans had really been feeling their oats, after the early rushes of success in Iran and North Korea. They finally got their shot at truly changing the Supreme Court in 2021, the year Ginsburg and Breyer both died.

It had been Trump's final pick, his fourth Supreme Court appointee, who'd made it happen, who'd really pushed it through.

Justice Dennis Rockman.

Rockman – the staunch family man, father of eight and fiery pro-life advocate from the great state of Texas – had been nearly eighty at the time of his appointment, and according to rumour, pretty much senile, but the Republicans had pushed his appointment through regardless. He was on the Supreme Court for just eight months before retiring due to ill health and moving back to Texas to tend to his hobbies – horse breeding and the Church. It had been the shortest SC appointment in history, but it was long enough for him to provide the decisive vote.

Anyway, like Roe v Wade itself, this was all history.

The upshot was that, two years later, when Olivia found herself pregnant, she'd wound up in the spare bedroom of a former midwife in Fort Wayne. The needle meant to puncture the sac holding what would have been Frank's only grandchild had also gone undetected through the wall of her lower intestine. Olivia had been told by the midwife (one Annie Baxter, who was still in prison, which is where Olivia would have been, too, had she lived) not to attempt the two-hour drive home to Indianapolis after the operation. She'd got an Uber back to her motel (the police had pieced all this together in the investigation) where she'd taken the strong painkillers she'd been given to help with the post-op cramping.

They worked all too well.

Olivia Brill, aged twenty-two, beloved daughter of Frank and Cheryl, bled to death in her sleep in a rented room off the interstate, due to complications arising from an improperly performed abortion.

Frank's steak arrived and, along with it, a tin bucket of fries and a bushel of mushrooms, sizzling on a cast-iron platter. He raised an eyebrow at the enormity. The waitress smiled and said, 'We serve our sides family-style.'

EIGHT

'He sure pissed somebody off.'

Detective Bob 'Chops' Birner whistled through his teeth as he ducked under the yellow tape one of the deputies was holding up for him. He was already out of breath. When the call came in and he heard the address, he'd made a point of getting here fast. There was blood on the front porch, where it had seeped under the door, and there, through the front door that opened straight into the living room, was the body. Old Hauser was a mess – his face pocked with a lot of little holes, propped up against one wall, the floor around him covered in sticky, dried blood. 'Gonna want these, sir,' the sergeant – Walter something, good guy, Chops had dealt with him before – was saying, holding out the little blue plastic bootees you strapped over your regular shoes. Chops bent over to slip them on – his arthritic knee giving him a current of pain, his huge gut tugging him earthwards, the very act of bending over costing him a fair bit of breath, causing his heart to flex in his chest a couple more times – and moved carefully into the house, a house he knew well, stepping around the puddle of blood. The forensics boys were busy bagging up tiny brass cartridges.

'.22s?' Chops asked.

'Yep,' one of the guys replied.

'Think it's a pro job?' one of the younger deputies asked, his reasoning probably being that he knew from movies and TV that professional hit men often used .22 pistols up close, because of their accuracy, relative quiet and so forth. But 'no', Chops thought, looking at the body. Looking at the number of entry wounds. Hit men don't get *that* angry.

Chops looked around the room, at the football trophies, in cases, on tabletops, on window ledges. He'd been in here, what? Four nights back? Him and Martin. Having some drinks, some fun. Looking at some stuff online. Not much sign of a struggle. Nothing smashed or broken. Shot him a few times in the legs. Torture situation? Or to neutralise him? Yeah, Hauser was old, but he was big. Got Chops thinking – *maybe the killer was old too. Or weak. Or both*. There was a wastepaper basket nearby. He peeked inside. *Guy threw up. Most definitely not a pro*. One of the forensics people – actually a woman, that blonde girl, the one he'd heard mouthing off about how great Obama had been at one of the Christmas parties – saw Bob looking in the bin. 'We'll be sending it off for analysis,' she said.

Chops sat his 230 pounds down heavily in an armchair, making a sound of pained pleasure, the way most overweight 63-year-olds sat down, and closed his eyes for a moment, saying a silent goodbye to his old friend. His closest friend.

So few shared their special interests. He opened them again to see the sergeant standing over him. 'OK. So how'd we get here?' he asked the guy.

'Paperboy saw the blood on the front porch, from under the door. Looked in the window and saw the body,' Walter said. 'Went to the house next door, called us at –' he checked his notes – '8.48.'

'I'll need to talk to him. We interviewing the neighbours?'

'As we speak.'

'And who is the guy?' Chops asked. Him and Hauser had enjoyed what might best be described as a 'clandestine' friendship. It was probably best to keep it that way.

'Martin Hauser,' Walter went on. 'Retired. Lived alone. Used to coach high school football. Originally from here. Moved back around fifteen years ago. He'd been living in Indiana. Seems there was some ... trouble back there.'

'How do we know all this?'

Walter handed Chops his phone, the screen showing Google searches for the name 'Martin Hauser, coach'. Chops pretend-scanned a few articles. Whistled as though scandalised. 'Yep,' Walter said. 'Goddamned pederast ...'

'There's a laptop in here ...' one of the other officers said. They stepped through into the kitchen.

Bright and clean, orderly. The laptop sat on a table in the breakfast nook. 'Have it bagged up and sent over to homicide,' Chops said. 'We'll have someone get into it. If the guy's an honest-to-God paedophile, who knows what's gonna be on there.'

Well, Chops knew. He had no anxieties there. He wasn't in any of Hauser's photographs. He wasn't fucking stupid.

'Detective?' The voice came from down the hallway. Chops and Walter walked on down and turned right into a bedroom, Chops doing a good job of pretending he didn't know where he was going. 'In here, sir,' one of the deputies was saying, one of the new guys, Tom or Ted?

They stepped into a kind of dressing room off the main bedroom. A big tallboy with a couple of drawers open. 'We just checked online,' the officer was saying. 'Seems Hauser had a permit for a Glock 17. But ...' He held up an empty holster. 'Can't find the gun anywhere on the premises.'

'Gotta assume the perp took it,' Walter said.

'Yep,' Chops said. 'Get the gun's serial number from the paperwork and put it out there.'

Chops moved over to the dresser. There was a photo album open on top of it. On top of the album a single photograph had been taken out: a boy, around sixteen or seventeen, in high school football uniform, and, next to him, with his arm around him, the former Coach Hauser, grinning, forty years younger.

'Walt, you got gloves on?' Chops said. 'Here, turn this over for me ...' Walt flipped the photo – on the back the handwritten inscription, *'Robbie M, Sept 1982'.*

'I guess this is back in Indiana?' Chops said.

'Jackson High.' Walter nodded. 'Place he coached. Think his past caught up with him, Chops?'

'He sure pissed somebody off. I'll get on to the school. See if we can track down this Robbie M at least. Probably worth going through more of these photos too ...'

Chops moved over to the window and looked out at the street. Suburban. Quiet, although a crowd was now gathered behind the tape stretching around the property, kids and stay-at-home moms, drawn by the cruisers and the flashing lights. Like most older policeman in major American cities, over the last thirty or so years he'd seen the murder rate tick gradually upwards and the areas where the crimes took place move out of their traditional strongholds – in Oklahoma City's case North Highland, the South Park estates, Woodward Avenue – and into other corners of the city. Was a time you might have been able to do something about this shit, back when you could still do some actual policing, really use your nightstick and your gun-butt and your fists to explain some things to the niggers and the wops and the beaners. Chops remembered his first partner, back in the late 1970s, old Sarge Furlong, big old Irish boy, catching that black kid shoplifting. Just broke two of the fingers on the kid's right hand. Swear to God. Like he was snapping off chicken wings. Sent him on his way. Never saw that kid shoplifting on their beat again. But that was long past. Democrats and liberals everywhere, even all through Oklahoma PD. It had looked for a time like the old ways might have been making a comeback, with the big man in the Oval Office, but now? With his daughter. Hell, she was a half-liberal herself, wasn't she? Couldn't trust her. Always pissing on about women's rights and shit. Bitch married a Jew as well, the first husband, the one they pinned all that shit on. Now that had been *funny*. Christ-killing son-of-a-bitch was in Rikers right now working on a ten stretch.

Still, Chops thought, snapping back into the moment, into the house, this wasn't the usual part of town for a homicide. And he had a strong feeling that the killer wasn't from around here. That photograph. 'Sir?' someone was saying. Chops turned. The deputy was on his knees on the floor by the bed, where he'd hauled out a big suitcase and opened it. It was brimming with magazines. Chops sighed and shook his head.

'Yeah,' Walter said. 'Fuck this guy.'

Chops was feeling a couple of distinct emotions. There was anger, certainly. The urge towards avenging his old friend. There was also, and this was probably winning out right now, fear. The fear that whoever had killed Hauser had done so because of Hauser's ... interests. Interests that overlapped with Chops's own. And that scene back in the living room, all those bullet holes. Had whoever killed Hauser found anything out from him in his final moments? Anything that might lead him to Chops? He was so close to retiring. Full pension. The magnitude of the scandal. He made the decision there and then.

He had a lot of vacation time accrued ...

NINE

'The love you take.'

Phoenix was experiencing a November heatwave — 25 degrees this morning. Somewhere around 5 p.m. the sun would drop and the mercury would rapidly follow it, tumbling down to around 10 or 12 degrees seemingly in a few minutes. But, during the daytime, it was *hot*. He'd sprung for a slightly nicer motel this time, the Tropicana, with cable, A/C and a pool you could actually swim in.

Lunchtime found Frank out by the pool, on a lounger, in shirtsleeves and shorts. Next to him on a little metal table he'd arranged mineral water, glass and novel. (*The World According to Garp*, a paperback copy he'd picked up in the drugstore. He'd remembered loving the book as a young man, but he was having difficulty getting into it second time around, he was having difficulty concentrating on anything.) He topped up his glass and lay back in the sun with thoughts of where he was headed, how many miles to drive tomorrow, how far up into him the cancer was now. Thoughts of where he'd been too, thoughts of Hauser, jerking and juddering as bullet after bullet hit him. Two girls, in their twenties walked along the side of the pool and established themselves opposite him with a pitcher of cocktails, cigarettes, magazines and ashtray.

No, it hadn't been any kind of fun, back there in Oklahoma. But, like the man said, hopefully that had been the bitch of the bunch. He thought of The List inside, in his bag in the room. Five names on it.

Now ~~(Hauser)~~ four.

Just getting tougher from here. Better strap it on. Suck it up. Buckle down.

Frank was soon ignoring *Garp* again as he found himself thinking about the reason he was here in Phoenix, en route to Vegas: his first wife Grace.

After he'd left her for Cheryl, Grace had tumbled into a depression. During this depression she moved back in with her parents and gained weight, sitting on the sofa, alone, ploughing through potato chips, candy bars, ice cream. One night, chewing on a toffee, she pulled a filling out of her back molar. This was how she met Dr Leslie Roberts, DDS. Roberts refilled her tooth. Then he asked her out to dinner. Following a whirlwind three-month romance, he asked her to marry him. 'Are you sure this is a good idea, Grace?' Frank had asked her. 'I mean, let's be honest, you barely know the guy.' Frank was told, in no uncertain terms, to go fuck himself. He was told that he'd lost the right to comment on such matters the moment he'd started fucking Cheryl. Fair enough, Frank thought. And Frank could see the logic:

she wasn't getting any younger, he had a good job, money in the bank, and he said he loved her. In the end, Frank figured, go with God.

It all started going wrong on the honeymoon, a trip to Palm Springs. He was rigid about his routines. He liked to drink. He liked to choose what she wore to dinner. What they ate. (Frank got all of this later.) What he didn't like to do, it turned out, was work.

He had very few patients. He played tennis. He went on long drives. When he was at home he rarely came out of his den. Thinking she'd married a rich dentist, Grace soon found she was paying most of the household bills out of the small allowance her father, old Tony, still gave her, Frank's alimony having stopped on her wedding day. Tony also staked the new couple three hundred thousand dollars so they could buy their dream home. (Leslie's dream home. He had, as Frank's mom used to say, champagne tastes and beer money.) Tony then invested a further two hundred thou into Leslie's dentistry practice. He was looking to expand, open up a second surgery. It also became increasingly clear that, despite his speeches during their three-month romance, he had no interest in having children. Grace stood it for three years before she asked him to leave. He flatly refused. He was perfectly happy here and if she had a problem she could leave. Grace pointed out that her father had paid most of the cost of their home. He countered that the money was gifted to them as a couple. (Indeed, as he knew, it had been classified as exactly this for tax purposes and if she and her father wanted to now say that this was not the case, well, Leslie wouldn't like to be the one explaining all that to the IRS.) After a couple of months of screaming and shouting about all this, Grace, on the verge of a nervous breakdown, moved back in with her parents for the second time.

Leslie established residence in the former matrimonial home and Grace and her father began expensive legal proceedings to get him out of the property, as well as trying to reclaim the 200K he'd sunk into Leslie's 'expansion of the practice', an expansion that, mysteriously, had never happened. Something else soon became apparent. While Leslie Roberts DDS had shown next to no appetite whatsoever for dentistry, what he did seem to have an almost inexhaustible appetite for were complex, protracted legal battles. It turned out that one of his best friends was an attorney who specialised in divorce law. He countered all of Tony and Grace's suits with suits of his own. He alleged that Grace had abandoned him. Tony and Grace retained one of the best firms in town, at eye-watering cost. After two years they ended up settling: Tony wrote off the 200K business investment and Leslie got half of the house. (The fucker even managed to keep all the contents. All of the furniture that Frank had left behind when he went off with Cheryl wound up going to this fucking dentist.) Leslie Roberts walked away with close to half a million bucks. After legal costs, what was left of Grace's half was just about enough for a deposit on a one-bed apartment.

She settled into it and started drinking heavily. Died of cirrhosis a few years ago Frank heard. He'd loved her so much when they were kids. Leslie Roberts took his cash and moved to Vegas, where he allegedly prospered in real estate.

There was a postscript to all of this. Intrigued by hints Grace had made about her and Leslie's sex life – or lack of it – Frank brought in a private investigator called Tab Leyland, a guy he used to know well during his days editing the paper. Leyland went to work. It turned out that Leslie Roberts had done all of this at least once before: used his dentistry front to meet a young divorcee – an Annabel Reed of Minneapolis – and then suckered her out of a chunk of money. Almost impossible to prove in court, however, Leyland cautioned. There was another kicker. During the course of compiling his report, Leyland spent a fair amount of time following the good dentist around. Tailing his car one night led him to a parking lot on a quiet stretch of lake road outside town. There, from a safe distance through a set of night-vision goggles, the investigator observed the subject, Dr Leslie Roberts DDS, enter another car belonging to an unknown male. An unknown male whom he began to lustily fellate. 'He's queer, Brill,' Leyland told Frank. 'Blows strangers in parking lots.' Frank never told Grace. *That fucking toffee*, Frank used to think. *If you hadn't eaten that toffee then you wouldn't have pulled that filling then you wouldn't have* …

The Computations.

But it hadn't been the toffee that had caused Grace to wind up childless, broke and dead, Frank knew. It was him. He had broken her heart. For the sake of experiencing a slightly different variety of orgasm with a different woman, he had driven her into the arms of Roberts as surely as if he'd introduced them at a party. He thought about the lyric from an old song, something about how the love you take was about equal to the love you make. Well, he might be able to pay something back. For Grace. For old Tony Deefenbach.

One of the girls across the pool walked past him and took a lounger closer to Frank. She smiled a hello, but there was nothing in it, she was just moving into the sun. It was the kind of polite, neutral smile you'd give to children or old people. Frank had been an attractive man once. Was it just that he was older now that girls never looked? Or was it something more? Was it rats who could detect imperfections and sickness in potential mates? Could she – oiling herself now, having slipped in earbuds – detect the cancer twining through him? Age, cancer, whatever. The effect was much the same – nullifying. You were a sexual non-entity. Come to think of it – when had he last had a hard-on? He didn't mind. It was kind of a relief actually. One less thing to worry about. Frank reached for the bottle of mineral water, poured himself another glass, and lay back, eyes closed as he gave free play to his thoughts.

What were the free thoughts of the dying Frank Brill, ex-husband to three women, father of two dead children and murderer of (so far) one man? He saw Hauser reaching towards him with a trembling, bloody hand and saying 'Please . . .' He saw himself with all the guys from editorial, clustered around the booth in the front at Macy's Bar & Grill, laughing as they overloaded the waitress with orders of Martinis and pitchers of beer. He saw himself hitting that great three-wood that time, absolutely pure, right out of the screws, flying nearly 230 yards, landing softly onto the green in two at the par five, then, naturally, missing the eagle putt. ('You didn't think you deserved that eagle, did you, Frank?' his playing partner – Doc Wallace? Tom Hunter?' – had said to him.) He saw Cheryl crying when he told her he was leaving her for Pippa. And he saw, as always, the primary images, the ones that rarely left him for long: the bodies of his children. Olivia in the morgue up in Fort Wayne, dead for three days, but looking so beautiful. The mortician had done a great job. Adam on his gurney in the emergency medical centre they'd set up in the aftermath of the shooting. (They hadn't let him look at what was left of Pippa's face – that last shot, to the base of the skull. He'd identified her from the birthmark on her hip.) His son, however, he ... he just looked like he was sleeping. Like Frank could have done what he used to on the rare mornings when Adam slept longer than them, just slip into the bed next to him and nuzzle him until he woke up, saying groggily 'Mmmm, Daddy ...' and putting his tiny arms around Frank's neck.

He opened his eyes, squinting up into the glare of the afternoon sun. He could smell tobacco drifting. The girl was smoking and reading a newspaper, a supermarket tabloid. 'IT'S WAR!' the headline screamed, next to a picture of President Trump. Not an actual war this time, of course. Ivanka had declared war on drug dealers, backing mandatory death sentences for offenders caught dealing at certain levels, stressing her support for the Accelerated Justice Program her father had introduced, a way of getting more criminals onto death row faster. It was said that she didn't really believe in it but that now, halfway through her first term, it was time to start riling up the base again, tossing them some red meat. They'd started dragging Dad out again at rallies, the old boy increasingly becoming a law unto himself, but loving it, all of it taking him back to the glory days of ten years before. Just the other week, in some arena in Houston, he'd slipped up and referred to a black man who'd been pardoned on death row as a 'fucking nigger'. The crowd had gone wild, gasping and cheering and applauding. It had made headlines for a couple of days.

Frank thought about starting a conversation, seeing what the girl thought about the headline, if she thought about it at all. Then he remembered he was in Arizona – Donald had won the state by a few points ten years ago. Then by a 15 per cent margin in 2020. Two years ago Ivanka got 75 per cent of the vote. He sat forward and said, 'Excuse me?' She looked over. He waved. She took out one of her earbuds. 'Hi. I was just wondering, about your newspaper there?' She looked at it. 'The headline on the front. How are you folks feeling about that here in Arizona?'

The girl turned back to the front cover and looked at it, surprised, as though seeing it for the first time. 'About executing drug dealers?' Her voice was high, almost shrill.

'Yeah.'

'I guess we're for it.'

'Right.' Frank nodded.

'I mean, we've got to do something.'

'Yeah.'

'If the president thinks it's the way to go …'

'You like Ivanka?'

'Sure. She's so beautiful.'

Frank nodded some more. 'What if you get the wrong guy?'

'Well, I guess that happens.'

'You can't make an omelette and all that?'

'Excuse me?'

'You can't make an omelette without breaking eggs.'

'What do yo—'

'It's just an expression.'

'I never heard that before. That's a good one.' She smiled politely as she put her earbuds back in and lifted the paper back up, signalling that the conversation was over.

'I had a daughter,' Frank said quietly, to no one. 'She'd be about your age. She died. They cut her inside and she bled to death in her sleep. In a motel room. I never got to say goodbye to her. We had our ups and downs but, you know, I loved her. I really did. She was my little girl.'

He could hear the tinny sound of the girl's music, the water lapping in the pool, glugging as it slapped against the filter intake. Traffic on the highway. A propeller plane droning somewhere off in the distance. Frank talking, no one listening to him.

TEN

'Las Vegas doesn't care for out-of-towners.'

The drive from Phoenix to Vegas took five and a half hours, taking the 60 out of town, then picking up the 93 around Wickenburg. Then north all the way up through Mohave County until you cross the Colorado River into Nevada. You saw scrubland and desert and mountains and rivers and gas stations and water towers. Frank saw a coyote eating something dead by the highway near Boulder City.

He checked into the Desert Pines motel (*'Hot tub! Water beds!'*) just after lunchtime and had a shower, washing off the sweat from velour seats. Nursing a coffee, with a towel around him, he took stock of his supplies situation, spreading it all out on the bed and doing an inventory. He'd been on the road for four days now and was down to two pairs of socks, one pair of boxers and a couple of clean T-shirts. He'd need a sweater too, was heading back north after Vegas and it would be colder. He checked the perishables.

Two cans of Diet Coke.

Half a carton of cigarettes.

Sixty .22 cartridges.

Ten 9mm cartridges.

He'd need more 9mm, for Hauser's stolen Glock. He was also out of shaving cream and deodorant.

In America, when your shopping list was as diverse as toiletries, soft drinks, cigarettes, clothing and 9mm ammunition, there was only one place to go ...

* * *

Frank parked, got out of the car and looked up at it, glittering in the hot afternoon sun, towering above him, casting shadows all around, huge, biblical. It might have been the biggest SupraMart Frank had ever seen. He left the desert heat of the parking lot, walked into the artificial cool of the temple ('*Welcome to SupraMart, welcome to SupraMart,*' the greeter intoned over and over, like a Krishna chant) and began to consume.

In the clothing section he chose a couple of check short-sleeve shirts, two three-packs of white crew-neck T-shirts, a jumbo pack of black socks, two three-packs of boxer shorts, a pair of chinos and a navy lambswool sweater. Frank marvelled, not for the first, but possibly for the last time, at all the things America needed.

The endless number of microwaves, blenders, toasters and TVs. All that milk. All those meats. Cheeses. How many different types of Cheddar could humanity need?

Trying to find the toiletries, he took an accidental detour down the baby aisle and spent a moment in front of the towering jars of food, diapers, teething rings, formula, toys and pacifiers. Man, how did anyone even manage to raise a baby fifty years ago, a hundred years ago, before all this shit was invented? Tears streamed down Frank's face as he stood there, remembering his children when they were tiny. No one paid him much attention. Just another nutty old man in Las Vegas. Probably had a bad night at the tables. This was the good thing about going crazy in America – there was always someone way ahead of you. Driving over here he'd passed a beggar who'd been eating an onion like you would an apple.

Pulling himself together, he got his shaving cream, his deodorant and his Cokes and headed over to sporting goods, where, behind all the camping and fishing stuff, he could see the wall of matt-black and nickel-plated rifles and the glass cases full of handguns, looking like specimens of an exotic, deadly species pinned out in some museum.

Like several of America's major supermarkets, SupraMart had got a bit jittery about firearms a few years back. In 2020, after the public outcry following the Coolidge High shooting, they had issued a statement:

In light of recent, tragic events SupraMart are raising the age for purchase of firearms and ammunition from 18 to 21 years of age. We will also no longer be retailing so-called 'assault rifles', including the AR-15. From the end of this year we will cease to sell handguns, bump stocks, high-capacity magazines and similar accessories. We will be requiring customers to pass a background check before purchasing any firearm. We must keep our children safe.

Now, six years on, things had returned to normal. Had indeed tipped the other way. In 2022 a series of Tweets by the president ('Failing SupraMart thinks it knows whats best for you and you're family. Un-American and BAD!') led to a sustained boycott by patriots that seriously dented SupraMart's profits and ignited a shareholder panic. The chain issued another high-minded statement . . .

We at SupraMart pride ourselves on listening to our customers. We are pleased to announce that effective immediately we will return to selling modern sporting rifles, including the AR-15. We will be lowering the age for purchase of firearms and ammunition from 21 to 18 years of age. We will also once again be selling handguns, bump stocks and high-capacity magazines. In compliance with new federal laws we will no longer require customers to pass a background check before purchasing firearms. God bless America!

Frank looked up at the wall of holsters, magazines, speed-loaders and other accessories. 'Can I help you, sir?' A sales kid, materialising behind him.

'Yeah, uh, I need some bullets for a Glock.'

'Which model, sir?'

'Uh . . . shit, I don't . . . this one.' Frank pulled the pistol out of the waistband of his pants and sat it on the counter. Even a decade ago this would have been bad news. But these days Nevada was full 'constitutional carry' (*'the legal carrying of a handgun, either openly or concealed, without a licence or permit'*) and the kid didn't bat an eyelid.

'Ah, the 17. We have a special on hollow points right now. Thousand rounds for $199.99 plus tax.'

'Well, I don't need that much. What's the smallest quantity you do?'

'Box of fifty for $32.95.'

'That'll be fine. But you're sure the ..., with the hollow points, that's, uh, legal, right?'

'Yes, sir. Since 2022.'

'Well, OK then,' Frank said. The kid started doing his thing, rifling through a drawer of ammunition. Something caught Frank's eye, up on the wall of accessories. 'Is that ... are they silencers?'

'Yes, sir.'

'They're legal now?'

'Since 2022.'

2022. Of course, Beckerman's bill.

'Can ... can I have one of those too?'

'I'm afraid not.'

Ah, Frank thought. There were still some limits. Some checks and balances. After all, why would an honest citizen need a silenced weapon?

'Not for that old gun there,' the sales clerk went on. 'You need a threaded barrel. But listen, I can do you a hundred dollars on trade-in for your old 17 against the new Glock 26 which is a far superior weapon and it comes suppressor-ready.'

'Suppressor?'

'Silencer. We have a great deal on the ATN 803. Very quiet. You'd definitely want some different ammunition to these standard 9mms if you're going for maximum stealth.'

'Stealth?'

'I'm assuming you want this for hunting purposes? Most of our customers find using suppressors very effective at reducing noise that scares off prey in a hunting situation.'

'Yeah. Hunting. Sure.'

Frank walked out of SupraMart with a brand-new Glock 26, an ATN silencer and fifty rounds of subsonic hollow points. Just a few years ago it would have taken a professional hit man many days, a lot of black-market contacts and thousands of dollars to put all of this stuff together. It cost Frank fifteen minutes and 620 plus tax. He paid cash.

'Have a *great* day, sir,' the greeter chanted as he left.

'I *will*,' Frank smiled.

* * *

He found the address with no problem at all, the voter roll leading him to a big, ostentatious McMansion on the north-west side of Las Vegas, in an area that looked to be only recently developed. Yeah, the fucker had done pretty well for himself. Pretty well all right. Frank staked it out, sat in the car for the rest of the afternoon, going up and ringing the doorbell, but no one was home. The light faded and, realising how tired he was, he started the car and took a drive down the Strip.

He'd been to Vegas once before, a golfing trip with some buddies back in the early days of his marriage to Cheryl. Frank wasn't a gambler, so it was all a bit lost on him. One of the boys had blown a ton of money at blackjack and another one spent a small fortune hiring two hookers, one of whom wound up giving him crabs. The dreaded side-walkers. But Frank had been in the early days of his marriage. He hadn't got involved. Vegas always reminded him of one of the last times he'd spent with Adam, when he was five, and they'd just got into watching *The Simpsons* together, sat on the sofa after he got home from school. One night it was the episode where Homer took Flanders to Vegas to try and loosen him up a bit and things went predictably awry. As they got run out of the city a security guard said to them, 'Las Vegas doesn't care for out-of-towners.' Frank had laughed and laughed.

'Why is that funny?' Adam had asked.

'Well,' Frank had explained, 'Las Vegas is all about out-of-towners. Pretty much everyone who goes there is an out-of-towner, so the joke is that he's saying something which is the opposite of the truth.'

'Like ... a lie?'

'A joke, son.'

'Oh, I get it!' Adam said. He really didn't, but it became a little running gag between the two of them, something to add to 'DOH!' and 'Thank you and come again!' *'Las Vegas doesn't care for out-of-towners,'* they'd say to each other, apropos of nothing, driving Pippa mad. Frank sometimes thought about all the little gags and catchphrases he might have got to have with Adam if he'd lived. But he didn't. He got shot in the stomach by a madman and bled to death on a classroom floor. And that was that.

He drove slowly along the Strip, bathed in neon, bathed in the money colours – silver and gold – and in red and blue, words reflecting off the windshield telling him FREE

BUFFET and FREE BREAKFAST and TABLE SERVICE and GOD BLESS OUR TROOPS, all of America wandering the streets beside him, craning their necks and looking at the sights the electricity had made. Right over there – the Mandalay Bay, where, back in 2017, Paddock had smashed out the window on the thirty-second floor and opened fire on the crowd below, over a thousand rounds, fifty-eight dead, the worst mass shooting in US history until Coolidge, until Coolidge was overtaken in 2021, when sound engineer John Urkel opened up at that music festival in San Diego with a Minigun he'd smuggled inside hidden in a speaker cabinet. He set it up overnight, on the mixing platform facing the main stage, undetected, and opened fire late the following morning as the crowd massed for the first band of the day, killing 139 people in a little over ninety seconds. Some of the victims closest to Urkel's firing line were simply 'vaporised' from the waist up. (Even the NRA's Beckerman was forced to admit that it was 'probably' unnecessary for most Americans to have the right to own a Minigun, a weapon designed for aerial combat and capable of firing 6,000 high-calibre rounds a minute.)

Why hadn't Frank gone this route? Full crazy. Taking his rage and pain out on an indiscriminate mass of people.

Because Frank had been the editor.

He was going to be precise.

ELEVEN

'I hope you enjoyed my sofa.'

The next morning, bright and early, just after 7 a.m., Frank was parked back on the street, watching the McMansion again. This time he didn't have to wait too long. At 7.32 a.m. Target #2 came out of the mock-Spanish double doors dressed in a flamboyant white towelling jogging suit. He was older, in his late fifties now, and much heavier than when Frank last saw him (what – nearly 30 years ago?) but it was definitely him. Frank followed along the street in the car at a discreet distance, pulling over and parking when the white towelling jogging suit turned into a small park. Frank waited. Sure enough, less than fifteen minutes later, the white suit re-emerged, running much slower now, sweat pouring off. Frank let him get a hundred or so yards along the street, back in the direction of the house, before he made a U-turn on the wide boulevard and headed after him, overtaking him and parking across from the house. Lost in his world of panting and sweat as he turned up the garden path the guy didn't see Frank getting out of the car. Didn't see him closing the distance across the street, his hand inside his coat. Didn't see him until he had his keys in the door and the door partially open.

He turned just as Frank was upon him, pulling the new Glock with the heavy suppressor on it out and sticking it in the guy's damp, towelling belly.

'Hello, Leslie,' Frank said.

Leslie Roberts's mouth went wide but no sound came out of it as Frank pushed him – hard – into the hallway (more a kind of large atrium) and stepped inside, taking the keys out of the lock and closing the door behind him. Roberts went sprawling on the floor – a kind of Mexican tile – and crashed into a small occasional table, sending a vase of flowers smashing down beside him. Frank stood over him and lowered the muzzle, the pistol looking huge and lethal now with the addition of the silencer. Sweating and panting, Roberts said – 'What do you want?'

'You don't remember me?' Frank asked.

'Leslie?' A muffled voice came from somewhere in the house. Roberts's eyes went towards the sound and he yelled 'JAMES!' just as a younger man appeared from a doorway across the atrium. He was in his early thirties, tanned, handsome, wearing shorts and a T-shirt. In his right hand he held a pitcher of orange juice and the words 'What happened?' were already dying on his lips. He looked at Frank holding the pistol, and then at Roberts – sprawled on the floor – and then he started *screaming*.

'No, please,' Frank said. 'Go! Just run!'

'OHMYGODOHMYGODOHMYGOD!'

'Shhhhhhh!' Frank said. Roberts was trying to get up. Frank pointed the gun at the wall near his head and pulled the trigger: just the clack of the slide and a pfffffft as a huge hole appeared in the dry wall next to Roberts and then the tinkling of the spent cartridge hitting the tiled floor. And now the smoke detector kicked in, triggered by the skeins of cordite drifting up from the muzzle of the Glock. *Beepbeepbeepbeepbeep.*

'OHMYGODOHMYGODOHMYGOD!'

'Shhh!' Frank said.

'HELP!'

Beepbeepbeepbeepbeep.

'PLEASE – RUN! GET OUT OF HERE, KID!'

'OHMYGODOHMYGODOHMYGOD!'

'POLICE!'

Beepbeepbeepbeepbeep.

Roberts, almost on his feet. A big, beefy guy. Frank pointed the Glock at his right thigh and pulled the trigger and now Roberts's screaming joined that of his buddy, the pitch, deafening, insane. This was a nightmare. There was no way out. He had to ...

Frank fired twice – *pfffft, clack, tinkle, pfffft, clack, tinkle* – the first bullet hitting the pitcher of OJ, blowing it to pieces, shards of glass flying, juice spattering onto the floor. The second bullet went through the kid's chest, silencing him, knocking him back and off his feet, sending him sprawling to the floor.

Beepbeepbeepbeepbeep.

Frank looked up at the ceiling, saw the white plastic disc, the red flashing light, and fired three times before he hit it, the beeping stopping, everything quieter now, just Roberts's sobbing and wailing as he rolled on the floor clutching his leg.

Shaking, nausea rising within him, his legs going, Frank walked towards the kid, who had managed to turn onto his stomach and was trying to crawl away. Blood everywhere. Frank flashed on that madman, walking the hallway of the school. 'I'm sorry,' Frank said. He fired again at close range, hitting him between the shoulder blades. The guy flattened down on the floor, his arms shooting out to the sides, all movement stopping instantly. 'Why didn't you run?' Frank sobbed. Somewhere behind him he could hear Roberts, throwing up.

After a moment, he joined him.

* * *

He had killed an innocent man. Someone who just happened to be in his way. This hadn't featured in his planning. In his mind he would find these men who had so wronged him and his family and they would be alone and they would confess what they had done and Frank would kill them and that would be that. Now, in the moment, surrounded by death and blood and sobbing and gun smoke, Frank thought about just calling a halt to all of it. He pressed the muzzle of the silencer to his chin, feeling it burn his skin but numb to the point of not caring as he moved it around, wondering which way to send the bullet. Straight up? Through his bottom jaw, then the tongue, then the top jaw, then up behind his eyes, through the frontal lobes and out through the top of his skull? Or thrust it into his mouth, feeling it burning his tongue, cheeks and the roof of his mouth for a split second before he pulled the trigger and it blasted out through the back of his head? He needed to ... he wanted ... a drink.

Roberts couldn't stand up. So Frank dragged him along by the hood of the jogging suit, the fat man sobbing and retching, past the corpse of his friend or lover, through the puddle of sticky orange juice and blood and glass, Roberts getting cut but not seeming to notice. By the time Frank dropped him in the middle of the living room the white towelling jogging suit was covered in blood and he was a hysterical mess. Frank flopped into an armchair, lit a cigarette with shaking hands and looked around for the liquor cabinet. It was a big room, with lots of plants and ferns. Jungly, almost. A wall of glass looked out onto a small, well-kept desert-garden. Frank's hands were trembling badly as he smoked, taking deep draughts of nicotine as he scanned the room. There were a few bottles lined up on a polished concrete counter that separated the living area from the kitchen. Ignoring Roberts's wailing and sobbing, Frank walked over and picked up a bottle of Grey Goose. He really thought about it, thought about taking a long pull straight from the bottle and waiting a moment until it washed through him, calming him. That old feeling of anaesthetic pumping through you, replacing your blood. He put it back, feeling the bump of the penguin in his left trouser pocket. In the background Roberts's wailing had quietened down, just muttered words now as he went into deep shock.

'Leslie? Leslie?' Frank said, walking over. 'Shhhh.' Frank put a finger to his lips. Roberts fought to get his breathing under control, taking lots of fast, shallow breaths. 'I'm sorry about your friend.'

'Who ... are ... you?' The words getting squeezed out through the pain.

'You don't recognise me?'

Roberts shook his head. Frank sighed and looked around the room. His eyes alighted on something. There, over in the corner, forming a kind of sitting area with two armchairs and a coffee table was a cream three-seater sofa.

Frank's cream three-seater sofa.

The one he'd left behind when he and Grace broke up. Frank pointed over at it with the gun. 'That's MY FUCKING SOFA!'

A moment, then Roberts said – 'Are you ... Grace's ex-husband?'

'I can't believe you still have our sofa,' Frank said. 'Why? Why did you do it?'

'What? I DIDN'T DO ANYTHING!'

'Why did you marry Grace if you were gay? Why did you take all her money? Wreck her life?'

'I ... I'm bisexual. We had a disagreement! We were getting divorced! It happens! We went to court, I won, and –'

'And how about the one before Grace? Annabel Reed in Minneapolis?'

This shut Roberts up. But he recovered quickly, blinking as he said, 'Who?'

'You're a con man, aren't you? You married a couple of women, got a lot of money out of them and then high-tailed it.'

'I don't know what you're talking about!'

Fuck it.

He closed his eyes and pulled the trigger three times, moving the gun up from belly to chest as he did so – *pfffft, clack, tinkle.*

Frank walked across the room and sank down into the sofa he had not sat on for decades. It was funny the way his body remembered the contours of the sofa, its exact, specific feel. He remembered the life he and Grace had when they bought this, from that nice store on Eisenhower, one of the first decent pieces of furniture they'd owned. Living in the little apartment, no kids. In their twenties. Just learning about things like cooking and decorating. Stripping the old paper off the walls and finding that old drywall crumbling beneath it. How the cost of the contractor to fix it meant that they were eating tuna pasta for two weeks. If you'd told Frank back then, when they were in the furniture store signing the papers (they'd been so broke, and Frank had been too proud to ask for help, that they'd bought it on interest-free credit) that before his life was over he'd own three different sofas with three different women, that this would not be the only one he'd eat his meals, read his book, watch TV, fall asleep and make love on, that, indeed, he would, many years later, get cancer and end up sitting on this sofa in Las Vegas with a warm gun in his lap, having just killed the man who'd become his first wife's second husband but who'd later turned out to be a homosexual long-con man, well. Frank might have asked you what you were smoking. But life was varied. Life was strange, he thought, looking over at Roberts's body, splayed on its back, a faint gurgling sound as blood continued to pour from its wounds.

Frank had hoped to get some answers. Really get to the bottom of why he'd chosen Grace as his victim. Ask him if he ever thought about the pain he'd caused her, about the fact that he was living here in this palace and Grace died in a one-bedroom apartment, her poor old dad dead too, broke and with a broken heart. Frank had wanted to ask Roberts about all this. But nothing turned out like you wanted it to. 'Well, asshole, I hope you enjoyed my sofa,' Frank said. He stood up and patted the arm, the arm he'd rested his drink on many evenings long ago, in another lifetime. The arm the TV clicker would often fall from, involving much heaving and huffing on your hands and knees because it would always – miraculously – manage to bounce *sideways* underneath the sofa. The way of inanimate objects. 'Goodbye, old friend,' Frank said. He poured the bottle of Grey Goose all over the sofa.

It went up with a gentle *whumpff*. Frank took The List out of his pocket and picked up a pen from the coffee table.

~~Leslie Roberts~~

He walked out of the place, several other smoke alarms beginning to beep crazily behind him, Frank picturing the house soon burning, all Halloween-orange and chimney-red, like the song said. Thinking about this in the car on the way back to the motel, Frank wondered about Mickey's Big Mouths. Could you even still get them?

TWELVE

'Uh-oh ...'

Every case needed a break. And the Hauser case might well have remained another unsolved, home-invasion murder situation had it not been for a piece of good fortune that came Chops's way one evening, a couple of days after the death of his friend.

He'd been at home, in his Easy-Boy, eating nachos drenched in melted cheese and reading some Clancy, Fox News on in the background like it always was. Well, he'd been trying to read some Clancy; in truth he'd been thinking about old Hauser. About some of the parties they'd been to. Some of the good times they'd shared. Two men bonded by a shared interest much of society deemed unacceptable. That time, with those two runaway kids they'd met in a roadhouse bar. Sixteen or seventeen they'd been ...

He'd been snapped out of his reminiscence by Fox cutting from a report on Vice President Hannity's recent trip to the safe zone in South Korea (where he'd caused some controversy by suggesting it was only proper that American companies should benefit most from the reconstruction of North Korea, planned to start fifty years from now, when radiation levels had fallen to the acceptable safe limit) to a breaking news item about the discovery of two bodies in a house in Las Vegas.

A neighbour had called the police after seeing flames coming from the rear of the property. The fire service arrived quickly (it looked like an affluent neighbourhood, hence the newsworthiness) and put the fire out before it did too much damage. In doing so they discovered the bodies of two men – a Leslie Roberts and a James Cuomo. Both victims had been shot.

The report then went into character bios of each victim, strongly suggesting that they lived what Fox viewers might term 'an alternative lifestyle'. Chops tuned in at this point. On the one hand it looked like the victims were rich, white (well, one looked to be white, the other was some mild kind of beaner) and had been attacked in a safe suburb, which was clearly an outrage. But, on the other hand, the tone of the report implied, these guys were obviously both fags so they probably got what was coming to them. Chops lit a cigarette and turned the sound up. Cuomo was twenty-eight and a bartender at a Vegas club called the Spike. Roberts was fifty-seven, a retired dentist and real estate dealer who was 'originally from Schilling, Indiana'.

Uh-oh.

Chops picked up the phone and dialled Vegas PD. After some runaround he got put through to a Detective Hartley. They got the formalities out of the way.

'Detective, I hear one of these fellas that got himself killed was from Schilling, Indiana?'

'Yep.'

'Well, and this is probably nothing, but we had a homicide here in Oklahoma a few days back. Victim originally came from Schilling too.'

'That so?'

'Yup yup. Could you tell me, was it a .22 used in the shooting?'

'Nope. 9mm. Glock.'

'A 17?'

'Hang on.' The rustling of papers. 'A 26 they think.'

'Damn.'

'And it looks like the shooter used some kind of suppressor on the weapon. On account of the muzzle stamps.'

'Muzzle stamps? So those boys got shot close up?'

'One of 'em did. The older one, Roberts. Shot in the leg and then took three in the torso point-blank.' (*Disable him, then finish him,* Chops thought.) 'The other one, the young fella, got one in the chest from a few yards away, then one in the back up close.'

Chops scribbled it all down. 'Shit,' he said. 'What are you boys thinking on all this?'

'Well, with the silencer, looked like it might be a pro job. But, against all that, whoever did it made a half-assed job of burning the place down. Apparently poured a bottle of Grey Goose over a sofa and threw a match on it.'

'What in hell's "Grey Goose"?'

'Designer vodka.'

'Dee-signer?'

'You know, expensive.'

'How much is that shit?'

'You got me. I guess like fifty bucks a bottle?'

'Damn queers got all the money, right?' Chops said.

'Excuse me?'

Shit, Chops thought. He'd overstepped the mark. Was a time you could say that stuff to another cop and not even think about it. Nowadays, damn liberals everywhere. 'Just kidding.' Chops said. 'No kids and stuff is all I meant. Thanks for your help, Detective.'

'Not a problem.'

Chops hung up. He was thinking, *it's odd a couple o' fellas both from the same small town getting whacked within a few days of each other miles away from home.* But – a Glock 26? Not a 17? And the silencer. Why wouldn't he have used it on the coach if he'd had it?

In the old days it would have been simple to track the recent sale of these items on the Federal database. However, due to a series of very public victories for Beckerman and the NRA in the last decade, it was harder than ever to find out about gun sales. Only basic identification was required for purchase. No wait periods. Very little profiling in most states. Basically, retailers had no obligation to report anything. If you wanted to know the history of a firearm sale you had to ask. And even then they could refuse to tell you. You had to threaten a subpoena. There was only one thing for it. 'Gonna have to do some good old-fashioned poh-leece work,' Chops said to himself.

Much later that night, alone in his office, a pot of luke-warm coffee and an empty Doritos bag on his desk, he struck gold when he cold-called the twenty-eighth Nevada gun store on his list.

Looked like he was going to Vegas. As good a place to spend his 'vacation' as any.

THIRTEEN

'Love it or leave it ...'

'We will soon be starting our descent into Washington Dulles. Please ensure your seat backs are in the upright positon and your tray tables are safely stowed away ...' Frank looked out of the window at the fields, already some snow in north Virginia. It would soon be December. He'd been on the road for over a week now.

First class was nice. (Then again, at eighteen hundred dollars for a four-hour flight one-way, it needed to be.) Why the hell not? he'd figured. Although, as he'd put his credit card down on the counter at the United desk at Donald J. Trump (formerly McCarran) Airport, he'd known it was a risk. His plan had been to drive all the way, but, emboldened by his early successes and exhausted at the thought of the three-day cross-country drive largely retracing the route he'd already taken, he'd cracked, abandoning his car in long-term parking and splurging on the ticket. Up here, in the nose of the plane, in the huge grey leather throne – picking at his shrimp salad, eating just a sliver of his filet mignon – he'd reviewed his progress and thought about what lay ahead, because, from here on in, as he moved from the personal section of The List on to the political, things were going to become exponentially more difficult. In truth he had no idea how much further he was going to get.

Frank had only flown first class once before, to Mexico on his honeymoon with Cheryl, his second wife. Now, descending from fifty thousand feet, nothing but water and coffee in his veins, eyeing the other passengers feasting on the remains of their wine, their Scotches, their gin and tonics, he remembered that week in Cabo. The pina coladas. The chocolates on their pillows every night. The fresh fruit at breakfast. The sex. The declarations of love. The talk of the family they were going to have. He went straight from that to the image of Cheryl's eyes, years later, blazing with rage as she flailed at him in the kitchen, telling him '*Get the fuck out! Out! Out! Out!*' Frank trying to shush her because Olivia was asleep upstairs. And, later that same awful night – nearly twenty years ago now, the night she'd found all the text messages – Frank remembered being in Olivia's room, his bag over his shoulder and whiskey on his breath while he stroked her hair, very gently so as not to wake her from her six-year-old's dream (what do they dream of?), and said, 'Bye-bye, sweetheart,' his voice thick, his wife's crying just audible from somewhere downstairs. When had Frank last seen Cheryl? Of course. At Olivia's funeral. She'd looked right through him, glassy on Valium. Maybe something stronger. He drained his plastic glass of sparkling water and ran through the Computations for what felt like the billionth time in his life: *If I hadn't cheated on Cheryl and we'd stayed together then we wouldn't have moved and Olivia might not have gone to that other high school and decided to do the courses she did and then might have gone to a different college and she'd never have got pregnant by that guy and then she wouldn't have ... and I wouldn't have run off with Pippa and then Adam would never have been born and he wouldn't have ...*

And, as they always did, the Computations came with the Images: his daughter, on her back with her feet in the stirrups, his son, on that classroom floor, trying to hold his guts in. What was he supposed to do with such thoughts? What was anyone? Frank chewed on a Xanax and went back to his notes.

Target #3 had armed guards at his home, because of the death threats.

Target #3 rarely went anywhere unaccompanied by bodyguards.

Target #3's office looked to be a stronghold, a kind of a fortress.

Frank couldn't see any way he could come close to getting in there. But, at the same time, the target had to get in and out of the office, didn't he? Maybe an opportunity would present itself. There was also, Frank noticed now, reading through all the stuff he'd printed off the internet, a museum attached to the target's office. In the same building.

He thought seriously about renting a car at the airport, but he knew that this would involve identification, credit cards, leaving more of a trail, further to the one he'd left at the counter at Trump. It was dusk now and he didn't have to be in Fairfax, Virginia, until tomorrow lunchtime, when he'd arranged to meet the guy from the internet – freedompatriot1776 – in the parking lot of a Denny's.

Also, he couldn't do much of his Fairfax research in the dark. He needed to walk the streets, get the lay of the land. So Frank took a cab from Dulles into Washington, telling the driver to just take him to 'a Ramada downtown'. Forty minutes and sixty-two dollars later he found himself in front of the familiar red lettering.

He took a room for one night, paying cash plus a fifty-dollar per-day minimum deposit for incidentals, and headed out to see his nation's capital.

There were lingering signs of the huge Veterans Day parade he'd watched on the TV at home: bunting hanging from trees, bleachers set out here and there along the route. A huge billboard, Ivanka with Donald behind her, both looking proudly towards the horizon. The slogan – *KEEPING AMERICA GREAT, AGAIN.* Frank took his time, his overcoat and scarf wrapped around him as he walked in the cold night air, heading west all along Constitution Avenue, the museums and the Smithsonian brightly lit on his left. He idled in front of a department store – the TVs all tuned to Fox, a story about the great gains being made in Iran, the main text saying '*TROOPS HOME FOR CHRISTMAS?*'. In much smaller letters, running across the bottom of the screen, '*Eight dead in Seattle school shooting*', the size of the type almost like Fox was apologising to its viewers for troubling them with such a tiny shooting. Terrible to say, but these words actually cheered Frank. Made him feel better about this leg of the trip. He'd come to terms with the fact that he might fail in Virginia. Or that he might die here. And now the image on Fox was changing again, as the anchor introduced the nightly segment by the Donald J. Trump dancers (and why weren't they the Ivanka Trump Dancers now?) and the quartet of blonde cheerleaders – in tube tops, Stars and Stripes hot pants and KAGA hats – started belting out one of their numbers. Frank could not hear the music but Fox kindly put a rolling banner up along the bottom of the screen so that he, and the viewers at home, could learn and sing along ...

> *Don't wanna hear from no liberals, uh-uh*
> *Don't care about their pain,*
> *We just love America,*
> *That's why we ride the Trump Train ...*

On the 'uh-uh' line one of the girls smiled into the camera as she wagged her finger. Frank pictured it, all across America, the screens glowing in the spacious living rooms of Florida mansions, in track housing in the Deep South, in snow-caked apartment blocks in Anchorage, and even in the Rust Belt of Chicago, the people moving their shoulders to the clunky hip-hop beat and singing along. Old folk singing softly as they ate tray dinners and clipped coupons. Little kids, copying the rudimentary dance moves in front of the TV, clapped and cheered on by adoring parents.

He made a right turn, north on 15th Street, the little map he'd taken from the lobby of the hotel held out in front of him like a real tourist, and he could see it up ahead, lit by klieg lights in dazzling white blocks. He walked on and got as close to the White House as he could, which wasn't that close any more. The safety measures. The clamping down on protesters.

Frank heard some chanting up in the distance and headed towards it.

There were only half a dozen of them (gatherings of ten or more without prior written authorisation had been made illegal by the Extreme Patriot Act), two girls and four boys, probably students Frank figured from their dress. They were chanting 'No more war!' over and over and waving their placards that said 'TROOPS OUT' and 'FREE IRAN!'. Their cries echoed off into the cold night, dying somewhere in the air long before they could possibly reach the White House. (Which, this being a Saturday night in winter, obviously contained not a single Trump, the whole family, as was traditional now, having decamped to Mar-a-Lago for the winter, right after the Veterans Day parade.) Two cops watched the protesters from about twenty yards away, chewing gum, looking bored, their hands resting on their nightsticks, their pistols.

A man came striding past Frank, almost pushing him out of the way. He was young, not much older than the protesters themselves, and wore a filthy combat jacket and a growth of beard. 'HEY! HEY!' the guy yelled, charging right up to them. 'LOVE IT OR LEAVE IT, YOU FUCKEN ASSHOLES!'

'Ooh, that's original!' one of the girls cooed.

'Why don't you suck this, bitch?' the guy said, grabbing his dick.

'Can I volunteer?' one of the guys said.

'Fucken faggot.' The guy spat.

'Guilty!' the guy said prissily as his friends laughed, taunting the man further.

Now Combat Jacket zeroed in on the one Asian member of the group, the other girl who hadn't said anything. 'Why don't you go back to your own fucken country, bitch?' Frank glanced over at the cops. They were just watching. Didn't seem alarmed.

'Fuck you – you racist piece of shit,' one of the boys said, their sense of humour starting to fade. Now Frank slipped his phone out and started filming.

'Fuck me? Fuck you and fuck your gook bitch, you fucken faggot. Here – gimme that fucken thing.' The guy made a grab for the Asian girl's sign. He got hold of it and they started tussling. 'Hey. HEY!' one of the other kids yelled.

Using the spar of wood on the sign, the combat jacket guy pulled the girl in towards him and headbutted her right in the face. The other kids screamed and jumped in.

And now the cops finally ambled over, taking their nightsticks out. Out of the them spoke into his radio out of the corner of his mouth, Frank hearing the word 'backup' as he stepped away, still filming. The cops started swinging their clubs, crunching them into the protesters, boys and girls alike, clubbing two of them to the ground as, with a screech of tyres, a police van pulled up and four more officers piled out of it, their own batons drawn. It only took them a couple of minutes to cuff all six of the protesters and lead them crying and bleeding towards the van. Frank, shaking, dry-mouthed, panned around to film the combat jacket guy, who was already staggering off into the distance, unharmed, un-arrested, chanting 'USA! USA!'

'Sir? Sir?' Frank turned. A cop, one of the original two, was standing there. 'I'm afraid I'll have to take that phone.' He was already holding out an evidence bag.

'What?' Frank said.

'Clause 14, subsection 11b of the Extreme Patriot Act of 2022: "*It is illegal to interfere with government officials performing their duties in any way, including unauthorized filming or sound recording.*"'

'I, but . . .'

'Hey, you wanna join your little buddies in the wagon?'

Frank handed over his phone and the cop started tapping at the screen. 'I'm going to need the passwords to your social media accounts,' he said.

'I, what? Why?'

The cop sighed. 'Clause 18, subsection 2, "*Officers shall have the right to request access to social media accounts of persons suspected of being members of Antifa or other known terror organizations.*"'

'What? You can't do that.'

'You wanna spend the night in jail? Talk it over with a lawyer?'

'I don't have any social media accounts.'

This was true. He'd had social media accounts once upon a time. He'd deleted them all shortly after Adam and Pippa were killed. The abuse and the death threats from gun nuts just became too much to bear. But perhaps even worse than the death threats were the attempts by some of these guys to engage in so-called 'reasoned debate'. These endless, circular discussions – packed with firearms minutiae and stats from obscure websites ...

@Frank14Brilly: You don't care that my wife and son were murdered?

@AmericaWarLord666: It is tragic, and I feel for your suffering, and I hope they catch the monster involved in this atrocious act.

@Frank14Brilly: OK. I'll keep my arguments for common sense gun control to myself.

@AmericaWarLord666: That's the problem, though. What more laws would have stopped this psycho from avoiding security, bringing a weapon into a gun-free zone and committing murder? All of those things are against the law, which criminals ignore.

@Frank14Brilly: You've convinced me. I'm glad the man who killed my family had an AK-47.

@AmericaWarLord666: Again, what law would have stopped this?

@Frank14Brilly: Not being able to buy an AK-47?

@AmericanWarLord666: We're still avoiding the argument that the man did everything illegal possible. Why are we blaming the tool, and not the monster? They don't have guns in the UK, so they kill with knives and acid attacks. More people are killed with fists and feet than rifles. Evil will do evil.

@Frank14Brilly: You might want to double-check British knife and acid death stats against our gun death stats. Again, why did he have an AK-47?

@AmericanWarLord666: It wasn't an AK by the way, it was a WASR-10. A semi-auto rifle that looks like an AK, but doesn't perform like one. Also made in Romania, not Russia. Not an AK.

@Frank14Brilly: What does that even mean? Is it better that my wife and son were killed by one of those?

@AmericanWarLord666: Again, I am sorry for your loss. But facts matter. The AK is banned in your state.

@Frank14Brilly: Why do we have more gun deaths than any other developed country?

@AmericanWarLord666: Actually, 2/3rds of those are suicides. Also, while legal gun ownership has risen over the years, the murder rate has declined. Seems like a good trend.

@Frank14Brilly: But, even if that's true, a third is still a lot. Why only in America?

@AmericanWarLord666: Part of it is probably that we have one of the largest and the most diverse populations in the world. We also have untreated and undiagnosed mental illness in this nation. There's a lot of factors.

@Frank14Brilly: You just want your guns, don't you? You don't care about anything else.

@AmericanWarlord666: We're just going around in circles. I will never voluntarily give up my right to defend myself, as Americans do 500k – 3 million times a year. And criminals will never follow the law. Again, I'm sorry for your loss, but facts don't care about your feelings.

This was all happening around the time Frank had lapsed back into drinking, so the discussion went on for over forty-eight hours, until Frank realised his opponent seemed inexhaustible, always able to come up with obscure data to back up his points. Always ready with graphs and memes to disprove what Frank was saying, what he saw on CNN, what he read in the *Washington Post*, when they still existed. Frank calculated that @AmericanWarLord666 had replied to him personally over three hundred times in the two-day period, as well as replying to the dozens of others who had gradually joined the public conversation. Even Frank, who was retired – who was pretty much lying around the house in his underwear drinking beer and vodka – had to take breaks for food, bathroom and grocery shopping. He mentioned this on a phone call to Olivia one evening.

'Oh, Dad, you've got to stop that.'

'But I –'

'Dad – you're arguing with a bunch of guys in an office block in St Petersburg or someplace. It's a bot.'

And so he stopped. All of it. Just deleted it all, as the cop was beginning to believe now as he looked at Frank and then went back to the screen, scrolling through the home pages on his phone, finding nothing, no Facebook or Twitter or Instagram icons. Finally, he gave up. 'Some kinda hermit, huh?' he said as he started filling out the receipt. 'I'm not going to write you up tonight.' *Write me up for what?* Frank wanted to ask. But he'd become aware that, having killed three people in the last week, it might be prudent for him to limit his interactions with law enforcement as much as possible. The cop handed the receipt over. 'You'll get it back in four to six weeks. Have a nice evening.'

He walked off towards the police wagon, whistling, the sound of the Chinese girl crying audible from within the metal walls of the vehicle.

FOURTEEN

'Manager of the Year.'

Chops drove out of the Holiday Inn parking lot in the mid-size Dodge he'd rented at Trump, the air conditioning cranked against the midday Vegas heat. Having extended his seat fully back, he still found himself with his knees crammed up against the steering wheel. It had been worse on the two-hour economy flight from Oklahoma City. But he was not a rich man and he'd been six-four since he was seventeen years old. You got used to it. Like basketball jokes. During what his phone was telling him was going to be a fifteen-minute drive, he ran through the chain of events.

Marty – shot at close range in his own home with a .22. Most likely a Woodsman.

His Glock 17 stolen.

A photo of a kid – Robbie McIntyre, someone he'd heard Marty mention before – from back in Schilling left out of the album in his closet.

The two queers, killed three days later in Vegas in similar fashion – home invasion, one of them disabled then finished off later – but with a different weapon.

The giant SupraMart lay flat and huge in front of him as he pulled into a parking lot the size of ten football fields.

One of the greeters took a break from saying 'Welcome to SupraMart!' and led Chops to the manager's office.

'Hi. Detective Birner, Oklahoma City PD. We spoke on the phone?' Chops was saying as they shook hands across the cherrywood desk.

'Ben Dahmer. Wow, you must have played some basketball?'

'Damn right,' Chops said, playing nice, letting it go.

He handed the guy his Oklahoma PD card. He was a little bit younger than Chops, in his fifties. Bald. His office was small and hot, up in the roof of the building, all those A/C and heating ducts coiling up below it. 'How can I help you, Detective?' Dahmer continued, sitting down and assuming a brisk, businesslike air.

'Well, Mr Dahmer, the member of staff I spoke to in your sporting goods department last night – Eric, uh Lowell? – told me that three days ago he sold a customer –' he checked his notes – 'a Glock 26, an ATN 803 suppressor and a box of ammunition. Some subsonic hollow points?'

'Yes.'

'Well, I'd like to see the credit card receipt and the identification they used. Also any CCTV footage you might have from that day of the entrance to the store and the sporting goods department.'

'You know you need a warrant for that?'

'I am aware of that, sir, yes. It's just –'

'Well, come back when you have one, Officer.'

And now Chops saw it, on a shelf behind Dahmer, nestling among the 'Manager of the Year' plaques and photos of him on hunting trips, the old red cap – MAGA.

Chops figured it was worth the risk. He took his glasses off and rubbed his eyes. 'Can I speak frankly to you, Ben? I'm investigating a murder back in Oklahoma. Fella who got killed happened to be a friend of mine. He was a good man. A veteran. Fella who killed him tortured him. Shot him all up to hell. Now, if I'm right, well … Oklahoma, Nevada. This is already a multi-state deal. Pretty soon we're gonna have the goddamn FBI all over this. They'll be all up in your store, asking for this and that, throwing out subpoenas like candy. And let me tell you something, those FBI boys will be more interested in protecting the rights of that pair of fags who got killed here than they will in finding the son of a bitch who killed my buddy.' Over a decade of Trumpism and they still hadn't succeeded in weeding all the Democrats and liberals out of the damn FBI.

Dahmer sighed and shook his head. He looked past Chops to make sure the door was closed. 'Deep state sons of bitches.'

'Tried to bring down our president.'

'Yes they did.'

'Failed though, didn't they?' Chops smiled.

'They sure did, right?'

'Amen.'

'You hang on a minute there, Bob …' Dahmer pressed his intercom. 'Mandy? Darling, can you tell Eric from sporting goods to come up here? Thank you.' He turned

JOHN NIVEN

back to Chops and smiled. 'You see the vice president giving them gooks what for yesterday?'

'Sure did. You don't fuck with old Hannity.'

After another few minutes of small talk with Dahmer, and then fifteen minutes with young Eric from sporting goods, and then another half-hour in the security booth reviewing CCTV tapes, and Chops was strolling back through the parking lot knowing much more than he had when he pulled up. He got into his car with two certainties, one photograph and one hunch.

Certainty #1: Marty's killer had come to Vegas and traded Marty's stolen Glock 17 against a new 26 and a silencer.

Certainty #2: He'd used these to kill the homosexuals.

The photograph: a grainy, distant black-and-white print of a CCTV still showing a man who looked to be in his sixties. Slim. Thinning hair. Wearing a sport coat and jeans.

The hunch: This guy had known Marty Hauser and Leslie Roberts from back in Schilling, Indiana.

Chops got into the Dodge and headed back to the hotel, where his laptop was waiting. *Pick up a bucket of chicken on the way.*

FIFTEEN

'You can't kill a Camry.'

Frank had spent the last couple of days getting to know Fairfax, Virginia, pretty well. He'd seen the sights – the courthouse, the town hall, and the famous 29 Diner, operating on the same site since 1947. (He'd tried one of their cheeseburgers, but couldn't get through it.) But most of the time he'd taken his coffee and his notebook and sat on a stone bench on Waples Mill Road, across the street from the huge glass-and-steel building, watching the comings and goings. He'd seen the target coming and going every day.

The bad news: the place was indeed a fortress.

The good news: the target was a man of habit.

Each morning he arrived a little before 9 a.m., in a blacked-out Hummer with two bodyguards. Each lunchtime, around 1 p.m., he left the building with a couple of colleagues, got back into the blacked-out Hummer with the bodyguards, and took a five-minute drive down the street to an Italian place called Beltrami's, where he and his colleagues ate lunch while the bodyguards waited in the car. They usually spent about an hour in the restaurant. Frank had cased the place thoroughly, eating there twice. The front looked onto a busy shopping thoroughfare. An alleyway out back led to a residential street.

He knew from his research that the target's home on the outskirts of Washington, about a twenty-five-minute drive from here, was out. It was a gated mansion, guarded 24/7. For the obvious reasons.

So here he sat, in a Denny's off the freeway a little way out of town, reading the local paper, the local paper around these parts being the *Washington Post*. 'NEW DIPLOMATIC TRIUMPH FOR PRESIDENT TRUMP!' the headline screamed, above a story about Ivanka's recent trip to Russia, where she'd been photographed fishing and hunting with the 74-year-old Putin, now in his fifth term in office. It was safe to say that it wasn't the same *Washington Post* Frank had grown up with. The original paper had closed down in 2021, after they had printed a completely false story they'd been fed about Jared and Ivanka's ongoing divorce. Kushner was in jail by then anyway but the Trumps – gearing up for Ivanka's 2024 run – had thrown all their might and resources into suing the paper. They won the case and the paper was forced to close. The following year it was brought out of administration by Rupert Murdoch, making one of his last major investments before his death. Frank finished the Ivanka puff piece and skimmed the rest of the paper, a hodge-podge of human-interest stories, celebrity gossip and relentlessly pro-government political pieces. There was one (small) negative story about an outgoing cabinet member, a practice that allowed the *Post* to brand itself as 'fair and balanced'.

Frank recognised freedompatriot1776 the moment he came through the door, because he was carrying, as he said he would be, a red umbrella. Frank waved to the guy and he came over and sat down in the booth.

'Just call me Bill,' the guy said, extending his hand, 'and I'll call you Ted.'

Frank nodded. 'Bill' wasn't what he'd been expecting. He was about Frank's age and conservatively dressed, preppy even, in a sweater, chinos and wool overcoat. Grey hair, tanned, healthy-looking. Black horn-rimmed spectacles. What had Frank been expecting? A grizzled vet. A biker. Someone with facial hair and tattoos in a combat jacket, someone not unlike the guy who'd butted that Asian girl in DC a few days ago. 'Just coffee,' this 'Bill' said to the waitress who'd appeared. She trotted off.

'I have what you requested, Ted.'

Frank began reaching into his coat for the envelope.

'Not here,' Bill said softly. 'In the lot.'

Frank nodded. Silence. To fill it, Frank said, 'So, is this where you do a lot of business, Bill?'

The guy looked at him properly for the first time. 'Are we making small talk here, Ted?'

'I guess so . . .'

Bill sighed as the waitress came back with the coffee. He took one sip. 'Meet me in the parking lot by the green Toyota Camry in five minutes.'

Frank watched him go and finished his coffee. Oh well, it wasn't like he was looking to make new friends here.

Bill was standing by the car in the far corner of the empty lot smoking a cigarette as Frank walked up. 'OK,' Bill said, walking around to the trunk. He popped it. The only thing in there was a blue canvas sports bag. Bill unzipped it and Frank looked inside.

'OK?'

'Well, I'm going to have to trust you,' Frank said. 'I don't really know much about this stuff.'

Bill closed the trunk. 'It's the M&P version. With the hundred-round drum.' Frank just looked at him. Bill sighed again. 'Pearls before swine. Listen, she's clean. Real simple to use too. I found you a manual online and printed it off. It's in the bag.'

Frank handed over the envelope. Eight thousand dollars in cash. 'How much do these normally go for?' Frank asked.

'About a thousand,' Bill said.

'Seems like I'm paying an awful lot of money for the car then.' Frank looked at the licence plate. 2012. 'Seven grand for a fourteen-year-old Camry?'

'One – neither the piece nor the car can be traced to you. Two – this is a Camry, you understand? I'm guessing you want reliable? You can't kill a Camry, my friend. This thing's got 150,000 miles on the clock and it'll go round again. It'll survive the fucking holocaust.'

'OK.'

'Besides, that's not what you're paying for, is it? You're paying for me to have never seen you in my life after you do whatever crazy fucking shit it is you're planning to do with the contents of the trunk.'

'What do you think I'm planning to do?' Frank asked.

'Ted, I do not know and I do not care. But, if I had to hazard a guess, I'd say someone fucked your wife. Something like that?'

'Something like that,' Frank said.

'You have a good day now.' He handed Frank the car keys and walked off, out of the lot and down the street. Frank called after him. 'Hey! Hey! Can I give you a ride somewhere?' But the guy couldn't hear him over the wind.

Frank went back to the Comfort Inn and spent a little while in his room practising, taking the safety off, getting a sense of the weight of it, feeling a little bit silly doing all this Travis Bickle stuff, but there it was. He was practising swinging it up and out of the gym bag when suddenly he felt faint. Weak. He sat down on the bed and looked at his hands, shaking.

He breathed long and slow, trying to calm down. There had been blood this morning, in the toilet. Dark blood. Black. Arterial. Not good. Eating him away.

He drank a glass of water from the tap, took two of the pills and lay down for a little while. How long did he have?

Usually everyone asks the same question.

Long enough, he hoped. But no sense delaying.

Tomorrow.

SIXTEEN

'frankgolf2000'

'Uh, can I help you?' Mrs Rosen leaned over the garden fence, smiling at the tall, heavy man in the fleece-lined denim jacket and heavy boots.

'Hi there,' Chops said, coming down off the porch towards her. 'I was just looking for Frank.'

'Oh, he's not home.'

'Damn. You got any idea when he might be back? I'm Dan. An old buddy of his.' He took off his glove and extended a hand across the fence.

'Rachel,' she said, shaking his hand. 'Rosen.' *Fucken oven-dodger*, Chops thought automatically. 'Not for a while I don't think. He said he was heading south for a while. He's got a condo in Florida, you see ...'

Chops had been working fast.

His internet research had told him that the late Leslie Roberts had been married twice before, one of the marriages being to Grace Deefenbach, who had formerly been Mrs Grace Brill, of Schilling, Indiana. Her first husband, Frank Brill, it turned out, had been editor of the local paper and a reporter before that, so it hadn't been difficult to find an image of him online.

Chops then came across the fact that he'd gone to Jackson High, the same school the kid Robbie in Coach Hauser's photograph had gone to. The same school Hauser had taught at. That he'd had his ... 'troubles' at.

The CCTV still he'd got in Vegas was too blurred to make a positive ID, but the two men did not look dissimilar. Chops flew from Vegas to Indianapolis last night and had been at Robbie McIntyre's mother's house first thing this morning.

He'd told the elderly, befuddled Mrs McIntyre (eighty-four) that he was a private investigator looking into the disappearance of one of Robbie's old school friends. Grateful for the company, the old woman had invited him in and, after a third cup of coffee, she'd led him to a closet where she still kept all of Robbie's things. In among the old vinyl albums, posters, schoolbooks and magazines, Chops found what he was after – Robbie's 1984 Jackson High yearbook. Sure enough, there on the inside cover, where everyone had signed it, was all the confirmation Chops needed.

'*To my best bud Robbie. Frank B.*'

'Damn, Chops, you're just too good,' he said to himself.

A quick look through the voter roll at the town hall had turned up the address that had brought Chops to this porch, conversing with the Jew. 'Oh. Not to worry,' Chops said to her. 'I just happened to be in town. Thought I'd surprise him.'

'Well, the condo was his wife's, I think. You know ...'
She inclined her head sadly.

'To tell you the truth, Rachel, we haven't seen each other
in a long time. Nearly twenty years ...'

'Oh goodness. Then you don't know?'

'Know what?'

Mrs Rosen told him about the incredible tragedies of
Frank Brill's life: the school shooting; his daughter's strange,
unexplained death a few years ago. (She didn't go into the
abortion rumours.)

Chops thanked her and left.

Ten hours later, at one o'clock in the morning, he was
back, sitting in his car, on the darkened street across and
along from Frank's house. Chops stuffed fistful after fistful
of M&Ms into his mouth as his mind drifted back to the
many stakeouts he'd performed, both as a cop and doing
the work he took on off-the-books as a private investigator.
The PI stuff was, on the whole, less high-octane, although
it was agreeably more salacious. He remembered the infi-
delity case he'd worked for that rich old Chink some years
back. He'd been married to some young white piece.
Goddamn race-defiling bitch that she was. Chops had spent
a week on her tail before he caught her on camera in the
house of an Italian-looking fella. Got some good shots too
– couple of the wife sucking the boy off, her on her knees
on the bedroom carpet. Telephoto lens from some bushes
in the garden.

Big old wop cock on him too, Chops had delightedly told
his own client. The Chink had burst into tears when he
saw the photographs. I mean, Chops had thought, what the
fuck do you expect? Marrying a young, white, American

woman and waving your piggly-wiggly little gook dick at 'em? No wonder they go off and get themselves some real meat.

Yep, all that stuff was fun enough, but it was nothing compared to the real cop stuff. That time him and Dennis and Marc had staked out that motel for them meth dealers. Three days before they showed up. All Mexican. All tweaked out of their minds on crystal. Dennis took point. Chops was second man through the door. He could still remember the moment when he got one of 'em full in the chest with the pump-action Remington, before Dennis had even shouted 'Freeze!' The beaner's blood hitting the wall behind him just before he did. Happy memories to while away the hours here. Chops checked his watch – nearly 1.30 a.m., the street utterly quiet and deserted. He slipped his gloves on, got out and closed the car door softly. He'd got a chance to look around the back earlier – before the Jew appeared – and had spotted an entry point. Moving quietly around the side of the property, moving with surprising stealth for one of his age and weight, Chops crouched down and started working his penknife into the crack of the low window. It yielded a little bit and he forced the blade up, popping the weak catch. With some effort, sweating and stifling his grunts, Chops pulled himself up and dropped down into the darkness of the house. He was in a laundry room: washer, dryer, a basket with a pile of clean sheets in it. He waited a moment, letting his eyes get accustomed to the level of light, then came out into the kitchen.

He looked in the fridge. Nothing much except a jar of hot dogs in the door. Chops checked the date. Close enough.

He grabbed a couple and chewed thoughtfully as he began his tour, working from the top of the house down.

In the main bedroom he saw that drawers were out and half emptied. There was no toothbrush or razor in the bathroom. The other bedrooms were full of junk: cardboard boxes and plastic bags of photographs and papers and whatnot. The sad detritus of the sad life of this Frank Brill. Carrying on along the upstairs hallway he saw the ladder to the attic was down ...

He went up it, waiting until he got to the top before turning on his torch. (Neighbours spotting torch beams strafing the walls of empty houses were one of the primary causes of burglaries being reported. Just ask Nixon, Chops thought. Good man. Damn shame. Whole country started going to hell in a handcart the minute they 'got' him. Took forty years to get back on track.) He stood at the top of the ladder, just his head and shoulders in the loft, the air up here far colder on his face as he ran the shaft of light around the dusty space, seeing the usual outlines of furniture and boxes, all the crap people took from home to home with them until they died and their kids threw it all out. He was about to go back down when the beam caught something on the floor, quite close to the hatch, something glittering small and gold on the felt floor. Well, not quite gold. Brass. Chops picked it up.

A .22 round.

Just like the ones they pulled out of Marty.

Hello, you sonofabitch you.

He pocketed it and headed back down.

In the dining room – computer, armchair, table, golf prints on the wall – Chops found lots of newspaper cuttings, about a school shooting, about the discovery of the body of a twenty-two-year-old girl in a motel in Fort Wayne. He carried it all through to the back of the house, stooping to pick up the mail from the front porch as he went. He sat down at the kitchen table and flipped through the envelopes until he found the one he was looking for – an American Express statement. He tore it open and saw what he was expecting – that it only went up to the end of the previous month, October. Chops thought for a moment. He walked back through to the dining room, staying away from the windows, and sat down at the table. Making sure the blinds were closed, he turned on the old PC. No password, straight onto the desktop. He opened a browser and, sure enough, there it was on the toolbar – 'American Express'. He clicked on it and the account home page came up, asking him for the password. Chops thought. An older fella like this Brill? Had to be somewhere.

He went through all the drawers, the bits of paper stacked in the in-trays. Nothing. Chops sat back and stared at the framed photographs on the table – one of Brill on a golf course with some buddies, one of a girl's high school grad-uation, one of Brill with a much younger woman, and a little boy, maybe four, obviously the pair that got whacked in the school shooting. He picked up the golf photograph and turned it around. Nothing. Then the next photo. Nothing. Finally, on the family photo, he struck gold – there on the back of the frame, in tiny, neat block capitals . . .

> Bank – *jacksonhigh1966*
> Amex – *frankgolf2000*
> IRS – *deathandtaxes1*

Chops tapped frankgolf2000 into the box. One card. Classic green. He scrolled through – last used ... United Airlines desk, McCarran Airport five days ago. Eighteen hundred dollars. Chops jotted down the details. He'd need to go through one of the boys back in OKC to get this. No way an airline was giving up a passenger's travel details to an off-duty, out-of-state cop. He replaced the mail, straightened up everything he'd touched, and was standing in the middle of the dark living room, preparing to leave the house the same way he'd come in, when he saw it, standing on the mantelpiece. An envelope, addressed '*To whom it may concern*'. Chops hesitated for a second, then sat down on the sofa and tore it open, holding his small torch close.

> To anyone left who might care about me, I'm sorry.
> I had my reasons.
>   Frank

He was back at his motel by 2.15 a.m., where he cracked open a pint of vodka and hunkered down with the stolen file, familiarising himself with the sad history of Frank Brill, former editor of the *Schilling Gazette* and murderer, so far, Chops was convinced, of three.

A few hours later, muzzy with a hangover, Chops was lying on his rented bed smoking a cigarette when his phone rang. He scribbled stuff down as he listened. 'Yup, yup, OK,' he said. 'Thanks, brother. I owe you one.'

'Chief, I gotta say, we should be sharing this with the Feds.'

'Yeah, we will. Just give me a few more days, kid.'

'You gonna catch this sonofabitch, Chops?'

'Bet your ass.'

'I think you will too.'

Brill had flown to Dulles. It was about a nine-hour drive from Schilling to Washington. Chops could be there by sunset if he got up now.

He got up.

SEVENTEEN

'... is believed to still be at large.'

The restaurant wasn't so busy when he arrived, just after twelve, getting shown to the table for one he'd reserved online the night before. Frank ordered a shrimp cocktail and then the chicken Parmesan. What the hell, might be his last meal. He couldn't really eat the rich food of course, just picked at it, sipped his water, his diet soda. There were a couple of kids eating lunch with their parents, over by the window. Frank felt bad about that, wondered briefly if he should abort.

Then a small commotion was happening over at the door as the maître d' – who'd greeted Frank neutrally – welcomed the party disembarking from the Hummer very effusively, showing the three of them to their usual table, the corner booth just along from where Frank was picking at his chicken. He felt one of them glance at him as they passed by and he kept his head down over the food. The place was beginning to fill up now, a lively hubbub of chatter, glasses and flatware clinking and scraping. Frank asked for the dessert menu. It was expensive, but that was the least of his worries. He looked across the restaurant and through the window, the bitter wind still whipping by. The Hummer was parked outside and he could just make out the two bodyguards in the front, one reading something on his phone, the other dozing, eyes closed, his seat back a little.

Frank slipped his earplugs in, pulled his gloves on and put the gym bag over his shoulder.

He waited until the maître d' was away from his post, showing a couple to their table, before he went over and, on the pretext of taking one of the place's business cards from an oversized brandy balloon, locked the front door. No one noticed.

He walked back towards his table, slipping his hand inside the gym bag. He carried on, past his table, walking right up to the corner booth. As he crossed the last few yards towards it, one of the three men looked his way and Frank knew from the guy's expression that he knew something was up. The man's hand went fast inside his jacket, towards his left armpit.

Not as fast as Frank's, whose finger, inside the bag, was already on the trigger.

He squeezed it and the AR-15 exploded, the muzzle flash tearing the canvas bag to smoking pieces, Franks's upper body shaking like he was gripping a pneumatic drill bullets spraying into the booth as Frank moved the gun a little from left to right, like he'd seen in all the YouTube videos he'd watched last night. The sound of the machine gun was *deafening* in the crowded room, drowning out the screams that had instantly filled the air, tearing the three men apart, the force of the shells at such close distance blowing big holes in them, slamming them back into the wall of the booth. Frank saw one of their heads just come apart.

In a slow-mo out-of-body moment he could see himself, Frank Brill, sixty-year-old retiree, standing there, teeth gritted, arms shaking from the force of the weapon, blasting away at three men he'd never met before in his life. Bullets tearing into plaster and flesh and into the leather booth, hot, spent cartridges tinkling onto the tiled floor all around him. It felt like it went on forever. In reality it took just six seconds to empty the hundred-round magazine.

Frank walked back through the room, the air thick with gun smoke. Everyone was on the floor, screaming and crying. A waiter threw himself down as Frank approached, shouting 'Please! No!' Out of the corner of his eye, Frank could see the bodyguards running across the busy road, dodging traffic, guns already drawn. He dropped the spent, smoking machine gun and turned right, jogging down the hallway towards the restrooms, hitting the exit door hard, running now, sprinting down the alleyway and onto the street. Somewhere behind him he could hear the body-guards hammering on the locked front door and then glass splintering as they started kicking it in. Frank made a left and slowed his pace to a brisk walk, his lungs aching. There was no one around. After a hundred yards or so he came to the intersection with the main road and turned right. There it was, parked on a meter, the green Camry. Frank got in and started her up. Just as he pulled away he heard them, faint in the distance, the crazed, excited whoop and gulp of sirens.

Forcing himself to drive slowly, he focused on his heart banging and clattering in his chest, the weightless feeling in his limbs and the nausea rising in his throat. Those poor kids, eating their lunch. Never to be the same again. They – fuck! Red light! Frank jabbed the brakes, stopping at the last moment, the tyres giving a little squeak, the car a little jolt, the motorist in the lane beside him briefly glancing his way. *Calm calm calm.* He wound the window down and inhaled cool, fresh air through his nostrils, fighting that nausea. *Easy, Frank, easy.* Suddenly the blast of a horn right behind him. Jesus! No, the lights had changed, that was all. Frank slipped her into gear and pulled away. Shaking and sweating even with the window down and freezing air pouring in, he found the freeway entrance and slipped into the traffic, just another American fish joining the great stream, the blur of vehicles headed north and south, radiator grilles and tail lights running against each other.

He took the 95 south, not stopping for over five hours, until exhaustion forced him to pull into a gas station off the freeway, somewhere outside a town called Florence. He filled her up and went on in, grabbing some coffee. There it was as he stood in line, blaring from Fox on the TV set above the counter, the newsreader (young, female, heavily made up, low-cut dress) announcing: *'And it has been officially confirmed that one of the three men killed in the restaurant shooting in Fairfax, Virginia, this afternoon was National Rifle Association president, Robert Beckerman. The police are hunting for the killer who fled the scene and is believed to still be at large.'* Frank looked around at his fellow travellers in the line, a trucker staring at the TV. A mom juggling her infant and her tabloid. A couple of college kids glued to their phones. No one looked his way.

He reached into his inside pocket, took it out and did his thing.

~~Beckerman~~

Three down, two to go.

'*At large.*' Frank smiled. It was a cliché he'd encountered many times in a career in journalism. Now it was him. He, Frank Brill, was at large. He walked outside and smelled the night air, yawning. Already a little warmer down here in South Carolina. He was tired. He'd find a motel for the night. Continue in the morning. Frank sipped his coffee and walked back to the car.

EIGHTEEN

'Shit, you're cold, Chops.'

Chops heard the news on the radio when he was switching channels, around dusk as he was approaching Washington city limits. A madman had killed Bob Beckerman and two of his colleagues in a restaurant near the NRA headquarters in Fairfax, just a short drive outside Washington. Obviously you couldn't get near Fairfax now – police, the media, every damn hotel booked up instantly. So he'd found a motel off the interstate, lugged the stuff he'd taken from Brill's home into his room and got to work.

He'd now reached some conclusions, stretched out on his bed in the early hours, working on his fifth beer and his third cheeseburger, glued to Fox on the TV, who were doing a kind of a retrospective on the great work of Beckerman. Normally of course the shooting of just three people – one under the threshold required to even qualify as a mass murder – wouldn't have attracted anything like this kind of attention. Why, just the other day there had been fourteen killed in Oregon (retired bank clerk whose wife had left him) and that didn't get anything like the kind of coverage the Fairfax shooting was getting. Then again, the Oregon incident didn't involve the head of the NRA.

A great man, Chops thought, taking a sorrowful pull on his beer. A great *patriot*. No one had fought more tirelessly for the Second Amendment. No one except the president. Not the current president, the one who had married the fucken Jew and who Chops suspected was secretly a bleeding heart liberal. No, when Chops said 'the president' there was only one man he was thinking of. *His* president. Her father. The greatest leader the nation had ever known. Would ever know.

He thought back to the Oklahoma City rally on the 2020 campaign, him and Hauser, one of the best times they ever had.

It had been a warm night, late summer. They'd taken Chops's pickup truck and got there early, hanging out in the arena parking lot, drinking beer, joining in the chants and the singing with the other supporters, all of them pretty drunk as it got near to show time. Things had been running pretty hot that whole election, the libs and the Dems and the fake news working overtime, trying to take down the president. The Russia crap. Then all the impeachment crap. There were protesters at all the rallies. Fucking Antifa, in their black shit, with their masks and their banners and their signs. Fat dykes and queers and all sorts. Obviously there hadn't been too many of 'em in Oklahoma – this was

Trump country, he'd go on to win 75 per cent of the vote there that November – but there'd been enough, a few hundred or so, being held back by dozens of Chops's buddies from the Oklahoma City Police.

Inside the arena it was ... magical. Hannity had been the opening act, doing his thing, winding the crowd up, getting 'em to fever pitch just as the great man appeared. Chops and Hauser had been right down the front by this point. When he came out ... bathed in silver light, his great, black shadow standing out against it, his golden hair shimmering ... it was like standing before your God.

And the speech that night, the blood and fire of it as he railed against the liberals, the scum, the animals, who were trying to defeat him, trying to cheat *them*, the people – Chops, Hauser, all decent Americans – of their rightful leader. He had warned them of the hell-path America would take if he lost the election, the dark age of socialism that would dawn, the food queues they would have to stand in, the weapons that would be taken away from them, the medicines they would have to pay for, for the bums, the vagrants, the immigrants. Chops had looked around him at the snarling, angry faces of the righteous – screaming 'LOCK HER UP' and 'FINISH THE WALL' and 'SEND THEM BACK' and 'USA! USA!' and 'EIGHT MORE YEARS!' – and grinned, basking in the hate, feeling the warmth of the rage, knowing that this was where he belonged, that all of America's history had been leading to this moment. They'd come barrelling out of the arena – 12,000 strong, inspired, incendiary – to see that black knot of protesters still there, still chanting.

The thin line of cops had parted for them without hesitation and carnage had broken out in the parking lot. Hauser had been old even then, six years back, but he'd been game. Chops had slipped his blackjack out and swung into the melee, taking down a kid in a 'Black Lives Matter' T-shirt from behind, and Hauser went right in there, booting the boy in the face as tear gas exploded all around them and shots started ringing out and firebombs traced through the sky. Chops remembered a few beautiful images, he deliberately committed to memory: a Negro's face, contorted in agony as he was tasered. A young girl, a ring of blood around her mouth, teeth missing, cowering as the nightstick came down on her once again. A teenage boy clutching a 'LOVE TRUMPS HATE' sign as he wept. The place looked like a fucking war zone and, for a moment, it felt like they could do *anything*. Just keep going, rampaging out of the parking lot, across the city, across the country, just scourging and pummelling, destroying all opposition as they went, carrying on all the way to California, sweeping every last Democrat, socialist and liberal into the sparkling Pacific, cleansing America for once and for all. He and Marty had stood there, eyes streaming in the acrid breeze, arms around each other, chanting 'USAUSAUSA' in victory as all around them the last dregs of the protesters were beaten, were hit over the head with wooden spars, with baseball bats and iron bars. It had felt like they were ruling the whole country.

'*THREE PROTESTERS KILLED, EIGHTEEN INJURED AT TRUMP RALLY*,' the *Washington Post* said the next day.

'*ANTIFA ATTACKS TRUMP SUPPORTERS!*' said Fox.

Chops came out of this golden reverie, tuning back into the here and now, into Fox – showing a clip of Beckerman's legendary speech to the NRA convention in Houston some years ago, when he took over from La Pierre, who had become a bit too warm and fuzzy for everyone's tastes to tell you the truth. Chops turned the volume up.

'And I tell you,' Beckerman thundered, 'if we do not introduce *mandatory* carry in high schools for all students over the age of sixteen it will be as though we are designating those schools as slaughterhouses. Abattoirs just waiting for the next Adam Lanza, the next whoever, to roll up and start killing. I do not say you are less of an American if you do not carry a gun. I say – YOU ARE NOT AN AMERICAN AT ALL! If you are prepared to walk our streets without the capability to stand up for yourself or your fellow citizens, then what are you? I say – *TAKE YOUR LIBERAL, SOCIALIST BULLSHIT AND MOVE TO ENGLAND SO YOU CAN GET KNIFED OR ACID-BATHED BY SOME CRAZY MUSLIM WITHOUT THE MEANS TO DEFEND YOURSELF!*' The Texan arena went berserk. Finally, here was a leader who told the truth, who spoke to the people in their language, as The Donald had done. Hearing Beckerman's words again made Chops almost tearful with patriotism.

He stuffed a fistful of fries in his mouth – reflecting briefly that he really had to stop saying 'yes' whenever they asked him if he wanted to 'go large' at the drive-through, but part of Chops always thinking it was slightly un-American to refuse such bounty – got up and crossed the room to where his gun was hanging in its shoulder holster on the back of a chair. He slipped it out and sat back down on the bed with the short-barrelled .357 Magnum, nickel-plated, rubber grip, his chosen sidearm of many years with the police department. A little bulky, sure, and with a big kick that made it difficult to master, but there was nothing out there with much more stopping power and it would never jam on you. You could, like they say, use it to hammer nails all day long and it would still cut dead centre every single time. Chops pushed the catch forward with his fat thumb and released the barrel, showing him the ends of the six fat slugs. He tipped them out onto the bed and picked up one of the bullets. He kissed it and rolled it around his face, feeling the cool brass on his cheeks and his eyelids. He snapped the chamber shut and pointed the empty gun around the room, training it on the TV (an anchor talking about the other two NRA men killed along with Beckerman), the lamp, the bathroom door. It had been a long time since he'd shot a man. How he missed it. The feeling of pumping a round into something living, of seeing it crumple and twist. That Mexican drug dealer, the *astonishment* on his face as he absorbed the load of 00 buckshot at close range.

He hadn't died right away of course. The boys had secured the room and Chops had come back and stood over the guy as he spluttered, trying to talk, trying to say something. Chops had knelt down close to him, listening while the guy sputtered rusty blood, unable to dredge up any air or words through his shredded lungs, his eyes darting about, haunted, desperate, their light already starting to dim. It was a rare privilege, Chops knew. To get to watch a man's soul leave his body, even if it was a Mexican's. Chops had fixed the dealer right in the eye and said, 'Looks like you're about to die, beaner.' The last thing the kid saw – Chops's leering, gloating face.

'Shit, you're cold, Chops,' one of the boys had said.

Hell, anyone would admit it – killing was a rush. Frank Brill hadn't killed anyone before Hauser, Chops felt pretty sure of that. But he was off now. Off and running. Getting a taste for it. Or getting used to it at any rate. To go from popping someone with a .22 Woodsman to emptying an AR-15 into three guys? Shit.

Chops put the revolver down on his thigh and turned back to Frank's file: newspaper clippings – mostly from what used to be called the fake news back then, before those fuckers all got shut down – about the school shooting in Schilling, Indiana. A bad one, Chops remembered. A bunch of little kids and a couple of teachers had got whacked. (If only they'd listened to Beckerman, who was quoted in one of the papers in Frank's file, in the *New York Times*, when he'd said of the Schilling massacre, *'How many times will the children of America have to lay such a costly sacrifice on the altar of freedom?'* a comment that had sent the libs insane at the time.) Chops saw that Beckerman's photograph had been circled in blue ink. He looked back at the TV – once again showing the grainy, distant CCTV footage of the man with the gym bag over his shoulder walking into that Italian restaurant in Fairfax.

Brill killed Marty because Marty had fucked one of his little school buddies.

Brill killed the old fag in Vegas because of something the fag had done to his ex-wife. Chops figured the second fag was just collateral.

Brill killed Beckerman because, in his twisted, crazed socialist logic, he thought Beckerman was to blame for all the guns, for some lunatic shooting his wife and kid.

Personal grudges and political ones. Who would Frank Brill kill next? The answer, he felt, was somewhere in this file. He unwrapped his fourth – and final – quarter-pounder with cheese and read on.

NINETEEN

'... lemme tell you, they're gonna get got.'

Frank wound the car window down, getting a good lungful of the warm Florida air. He'd spent the night at a place called Jimmy's Cabins (*'waterbeds'*, *'HBO'*) and got on the road early, just after 7 a.m. It had been years since he'd been down here.

They used to spend part of every winter at the condo, before Adam went to school. They'd even talked about moving here at one point, but Frank had felt that the whole thing – Florida, golf, the beach every day – would have been too much like being a proper retiree and he wasn't quite ready for that at the time. Another apparently tiny decision that had cost him so very dearly. (The Computations: *If they'd moved here then Pippa and Adam would never have gone to that school and then ...*) He watched the familiar territory roll past – the lakes, the reeds, signs warning of gators, all under clear skies and warm sun. He'd rung Brock

('Mr Schmidt' Frank had almost called him, old habits dying hard, the man having owned the paper for all that time Frank and his father worked for it) first thing that morning, from the motel – telling him he was down for a few days, would be great to catch up – and had been invited over for dinner that evening.

Frank took the exit for Lake Tranquil.

He put the car in the underground lot – an ache in his heart as he remembered that short, blissful time when they'd do this every winter with Adam, the little boy usually asleep in the back when they pulled in here after two days on the road – got his bag and the groceries out the trunk and rode the elevator up to 14.

He opened the door and was stunned at how the condo had refused to change in the – what? – five years since he'd last been here. They (well, he) paid a caretaking company who came in twice a month, to vacuum and dust and check the place was OK, to turn the heat on sometimes if it got too cold in what passed for winter in Florida. Frank and Pippa had inherited the modest two-bedroom after Pippa's mom passed and Pippa had spruced it up, repainting the yellow walls a cool, neutral grey, replacing the 1980s peach and mint-green floral sofas in the living room – the room Frank was standing in now, dropping his car keys into the wooden bowl by the door – with a matching pair from Crate & Barrel, navy blue with white piping. She'd found the oak coffee table that sat between the sofas at a swap meet over in Kissimmee one Sunday morning. (Frank remembered the day, sitting feeding two-year-old Adam some ice cream in the shade while Pippa scoured the stalls.) She'd replaced the faded linoleum on the floor of the small galley kitchen – the kitchen Frank was popping his head into now – with sand-coloured stone tiles.

He opened the fridge: some beers, a bottle of still mineral water. Various condiments. All long out of date. Frank threw it all in the trash and started unloading the groceries he'd bought at the gas station on the 95. A six-pack of 7-Up, a couple of microwave pasta things, milk, coffee, a half-pound of butter, half a dozen eggs. He knew he had to try and eat something (his belt was ratcheted up to the last hole now and was still hanging loose), so he left a jar of mayo, some American cheese, a pack of ham and a loaf of white bread on the little round dining table. It'd been a bit of a grab bag, grocery-wise. It was difficult to shop for food when you just weren't hungry and, besides, he wasn't sure how long he was going to be here. That'd depend on how it went tonight, with Mr Schmidt. Shit, with *Brock*. He slathered mayo onto bread and stuffed a couple of slices of ham and cheese on there before topping with another slice of bread. He opened one of the 7-Ups and took his lunch back through the living room and out onto the balcony – the apartment's best feature.

He sipped his soda and looked out over the lake, hearing the buzz of jet skis, seeing families and couples strolling on the boardwalk across the road. It was strange. In his memory he'd done exactly this often, stood out on the balcony having a soda (well, a beer in the early days) and a smoke as soon as they'd got here, although back then there would have been the noise of a toddler running around, a wife in the kitchen, unpacking groceries, the TV already on, showing cartoons. In reality it had only maybe been half a dozen times in the five years of Adam's life. Their time together had really been so very short.

After he'd finished his drink and managed to take a few bites of the sandwich, Frank got up, went back inside, and turned on Fox.

After an item about the wall (construction problems being overcome heroically) and one on the economy (things were going great, apparently there was no need to worry about the deficit now being seven trillion dollars) there was an update on the Fairfax shooting. There were interviews with NRA members (*'whoever did this, lemme tell you, they're gonna get got'*) and a screenshot of a tweet from Ivanka: 'Bob Beckerman was a great American who fought tirelessly for the Second Amendment. We will find his killer!' Then the anchor was saying *'Police have released images of . . .'* and a CCTV photo of Frank came up. It was blurred, taken at some distance – clearly from a camera on the street outside the restaurant – and showed Frank arriving, with the canvas gym bag over his shoulder. He had sunglasses on and you couldn't really tell if it was him or not. *'He is described as being in his sixties, slim, with dark hair. He is considered to be armed and dangerous . . .'* Frank turned the volume down. Of course he'd been listening to updates in the car on the way down here. Had read all of that morning's papers over breakfast. It seemed like this was all they had – just a bad photograph. No lead on his name, or the car or anything like that. *'And the National Rifle Association,'* the Fox anchor was saying now, *'has just announced that it is posting a reward of half a million dollars for information leading to the arrest of the killer of Bob Beckerman and his associates. We go live now to NRA spokesperson . . .'* So it was official — Frank was a wanted man. There was a price on his head.

He laughed.

The only thing in the living room that was authentically Frank was the old brown leather Barcalounger by the glass doors onto the balcony. It had belonged to Pippa's father and Frank had insisted it stayed, over her protests. *Now this is comfy*, he thought as he lowered himself into it and flipped the lever extending the footrest.

'You look like such an old man in that damn chair,' she'd say.

'I am *an old man,'* he'd say.

He checked his watch — a little after two. Plenty of time for a nap before the ninety-minute drive down to West Palm Beach. Frank Brill dropped off quickly, exhausted from the drive, enjoying the lake breeze wafting in the open balcony doors, falling swiftly into a dream where he was eating a hot dog over on the beach across the street, feeding pieces of it to his dead son, his dead wife some-where close by, somewhere on the edge of the picture.

* * *

He woke up with a start, a little over an hour later, and took a shower. This wound up taking longer than expected because, when he'd pulled the shower curtain back to turn it on, he saw something he'd completely forgotten would still be there — a mesh net bag filled with Adam's little plastic bath toys, stuck to the tiled wall with suction cups. His little boats, ducks and the small penguin Frank used to make 'walk the plank' along the edge of the bath before dropping it with a scream into the water. (*'Again! Again,*

Daddy!') Well, after taking that in he'd spent a while sobbing on the bathroom floor. It took half a Xanax to pull himself together again, with the result that it was nearly five when he got on the road south, so it was almost six thirty, getting dark, when Frank pulled into the Schmidts' street in Prospect Park.

Safe to say the area was somewhat more high-end than Frank's Florida home: big mansions, mostly built in the 1920s, separated by palm trees and tall hedges, with 'armed response' signs on the front lawns. This was West Palm Beach, not quite as chic and affluent as its eastern neighbour right on the Atlantic, but getting there these days, especially during the last decade or so as the First Family had made the area their official home from October through to April.

Frank pulled up to the wrought-iron gate and leaned out of the car to press the buzzer on the little metal box set on a pole. 'Can I help you?' the voice said.

'Hi. Frank Brill. I'm here to see —'

'Of course, Mr Brill. One moment ...'

A click and a buzz and the heavy gate was swinging open in front of him. Frank drove onto the gravel and parked in front. He took a couple of deep breaths. In the main he managed to avoid anyone from his old life (well, his *life* would be a better way of putting it) because their sympathy was the hardest thing of all to bear. But it had to be done. It was necessary for the final act, if he ever got that far. Brock was already on the doorstep by the time Frank got out of the car. 'Frank!' he said, coming towards him, beaming. 'What a pleasant surprise!' They shook hands.

'Hi, Brock,' Frank said, taking in his former boss for the first time since the twin funeral for his wife and son.

Schmidt had to be nearly eighty now, but he looked to be in better shape than Frank, with a nice, even, year-round tan, perfect white teeth, still trim in his chinos and polo shirt. 'You're looking well.'

'Oh hell, I'm getting older and dumber by the day, Frank. But how are you?' Frank smiled weakly and shrugged, as if to say 'somehow I'm still here'. Brock just nodded and gripped Frank's shoulder tightly. A nice gesture, Frank thought. It said, *We know what you've been through and you don't have to talk about it if you don't want to.* He knew they'd have heard about Olivia from back home. They might well have sent a card, but Frank didn't remember much from that time. He'd already decided he wouldn't be telling them about the cancer. Really, what was the point? 'Well, come in, come in,' Brock was saying. 'Cyn's in the kitchen. She's dying to see you again ...'

Frank had only been in this house once before, on a visit with Pippa and Adam, but he remembered its scents immediately: lots of wood – the mahogany panelling, the polished floors – mixing with sweet potpourri, fresh-cut flowers from the garden, Brock's cologne, citrus trees and, somewhere off in the distance, cooking. The scents of rich, retired America.

As they walked through the big, airy lounge, Cynthia Brock came through the door at the far end to greet them. 'Frank!' she trilled. 'How lovely to see you again!' She was smiling, but the eyes were crinkled with sorrow. Combined with the slight head tilt as she reached him, it was the female version of that shoulder grip Brock had just given him, a look that said, *We know what you've been through, you poor man.* Cynthia embraced him, the smell of perfume and the onions she'd been chopping adding to the olfactory symphony.

'Hello, Cynthia,' Frank said. 'Something smells good.'

'Oh, it's just some lamb. I'm nearly done in there. Brock, I thought we'd eat outside. Do you want to take Frank out for a drink? I'll let you boys catch up for a bit then I'll join you.'

'Do you need any help in the kitchen?' Frank asked.

'You see,' Cynthia said, looking at her husband. 'Manners. I don't think I've heard that sentence once from you in forty years, Brock Schmidt.'

'Don't be holding out for it any time soon. Come on through, Frank ...'

He followed his host out onto the back patio, a terrace overlooking the lush garden and small pool (Frank remembering Adam splashing in it), the pool lit from beneath, the water shimmering mint green in the gathering dusk, lamps glowing throughout the shrubbery, candles already flickering on the wooden table set for three.

'What's your poison, Frank?' Brock asked, walking towards the full wet bar beside the pool.

'Just a Coke,' Frank said.

'Off the sauce, huh?'

'Yeah, something like that. Nah, just a long drive back. Not as sharp as I used to be!'

'I hear that ...' Brock was letting it go. Some people you hadn't seen in a while, you told them you didn't drink any more, it was like you'd told *them* they couldn't drink any more. Or at least told them they shouldn't. That they were fucking losers if they did. Brock took a Coke and a bottle of white wine from a small, glass-fronted fridge and poured them both a drink. They settled on two armchairs. 'Cheers,' Brock said.

Frank waited for it.

'Look, Frank.' He lowered his voice and glanced towards the house, conspiratorially, as though he wanted to get this over with, man-to-man. 'I don't have to tell you how sorry we were to hear about Olivia. It's just ... crazy. After all that's happened to you already. I can't imagine what you've been through, son.' That 'son'. Mr Schmidt, as he was back then, had been in his late thirties when Frank joined the paper as a teenager. Frank nodded along. It was surreal, being with people. Making conversation. He did it so very rarely nowadays. He took a deep draught of the coke. Maybe he should have had a drink. He fished in his pocket for the penguin, but he'd left it in his other pants.

'It's been tough,' Frank said. 'But it's been three years now. Time helps.'

'Of course.'

They sipped their drinks.

'And you're staying at the condo?' Frank nodded. 'How long are you here for?'

'A couple of weeks. Getting so cold back home now. You'll remember that ...'

'I sure do.' Brock shuddered. 'You should stay longer. You're retired now. We can play some golf. Been a long time since the two of us had a round.'

It had come up so quickly. Frank had thought he might have had to work the conversation around to it. Now he might even be able to get out of here early. Fake a headache, or exhaustion from the drive or something. 'I'd like that,' Frank said. 'How's your game?'

'Hell, I'm struggling off the tee. You wait till you're my age. Just no power left, Frank. Can't get through the ball like I used to.' Brock mimed the rotation. Frank remembered his swing from their time at the country club back home. In his day the old man used to hit a high, powerful draw.

'Oh, I'm the same,' Frank said. 'Played with some kids at the club back in the summer,' he lied. 'The *distance* they hit the damn ball. 310. 320.'

'I know, it's crazy, right?'

'Hitting five-irons over two hundred yards.'

'That was a decent drive back when I started playing!' Brock said. 'You know, I was watching this kid on TV recently. He's got something like 250 to carry, so ...'

Brock talked on as he poured himself more wine and Frank relaxed. They were men now, men on the safe, hallowed ground of sport, where all the talk was of yardages, statistics, form, technique. Where it was all facts. And facts, as @AmericanWarlord666 had delighted in telling Frank, didn't care about his feelings. Which suited him. Finally, Frank said, 'So, how about tomorrow?'

'Tomorrow ... tomorrow ...' Brock said, thinking. He probably already had plans, but Frank was gambling that a combination of factors – the fact that they hadn't seen each other in years, that Frank had been through such unimaginable pain – would pull in his favour.

'Is it difficult to get in?' Frank asked. 'With all the security, I mean?'

'Nah, it's fine. They're not in residence at the moment.' Frank already knew this, from his research. They were in El Paso, for some wall extension ceremony. 'It's a whole other story when they are there though. You get your car searched, your golf bag X-rayed, the whole nine yards. Even the members.'

'Wow.' Although Frank knew this too, from his research.

'Well, you can't be too careful these days. Christ, look what happened in Fairfax the other day ...'

'Yeah, I saw that ...'

'You know what – I can move a couple of things around. Have to be the afternoon though.'

'Fine by me,' Frank said. 'My schedule is ... light.'

'Right, you're on. I'll see if I can get us out around one o'clock, OK? Meet you at the club at twelve and we can have a coffee?'

'Great, thanks, Brock.'

Cynthia appeared, heavily made up and having changed into a billowing white dress, saying, 'Let's eat, boys,' and they moved over to the table.

Their maid served the food Cynthia had prepared and Frank let the nice old couple talk at him – of grandchildren and vacations and helping the kids out with mortgage deposits and interest rates and school fees and what Ivanka wore to the opening ceremony for the new stretch of wall and how, yes, Vice President Hannity said some really awful things but his bark was worse than his bite and if they didn't want to live in cages they shouldn't try and come into the country illegally and everyone knew but lord Cyn found it hard to watch the footage of those little kids all locked up – while he managed to chew his way through the fat, juicy shrimp and shredded lettuce and then the rare lamb cutlets with lima beans and fondant potatoes, the hosts moving from Sancerre to a Cabernet, and finally to a

Sauterne with the Key lime pie (Frank staying with the soda and then coffee, thinking often of his little penguin), and then he was hugging them and saying what a wonderful evening he'd had and that he'd see Brock at the golf course the next day and he'd hopefully see Cynthia real soon and then he was in his car waving as he crunched back out of the gravel drive.

TWENTY

'Taking dinner home for the family?'

Chops packing, fast.

Two days in Fairfax, Virginia, had got him nowhere. His out-of-state credentials cut no ice up here. The local cops were reluctant to share anything, even in the way of gossip. He'd hung around, talking to some of the NRA supporters, kindred spirits. There were hundreds of them, mounting a vigil outside the headquarters, just along the road from the restaurant where it happened. The restaurant itself was still a major crime scene, but Chops had been able to walk around the nearby streets and get a feel for how Brill had done it. He'd locked the front door, gone out the back way. The back door of the restaurant opened onto an alleyway that gave out onto a residential street. It was a dead end to the right, opened onto a main road to the left. *He'd have left his car there. Down the alleyway, boom, in and off in two minutes.* No CCTV cameras on that part of the main road either. Just that one grainy, distant shot of Brill entering the place. Chops hit the pavement, talking to store owners, householders and what have you. He hit the local landmarks, like the 49 Diner (where he'd tried one of their famous cheeseburgers. It was for shit. Somehow too ... organic, too natural-tasting for Chops's palate, accustomed as it was to the Colonel, Ronald and the Burger King), but ... nothing. Local cops had already been around of course. No one saw anything. Knew anything.

For an amateur this guy came and went like a fucking ghost.

The file was a bust too – no leads on where he might be headed next. Chops had only one card to play but it seemed like such a long shot it wasn't even worth bothering with.

On his second night, last night, Chops had been about ready to throw the towel in. This was deep, multi-state shit now. All that mattered was getting the guy. Fuck it – he was going to go to the FBI and tell them everything he knew, starting with Hauser and then the fags in Vegas, how Chops had put them together.

When it came to Beckerman, well, he was going to have to bullshit there. He could just about play the 'rogue cop following a hunch' card up to and including his visit to the Vegas SupraMart, but, after that ... breaking and entering a private citizen's home? Logging into their credit card account? Stealing their papers? Yeah, that wouldn't fly. He'd call Donnie Chong in the morning, the Chink he knew over at FBI field office in Oklahoma City.

And that had been Chops's plan last night, as he sat in front of the TV in his motel room, working his way through a ten-piece bucket, four fries, beans, gravy and a quart of Coke. ('Taking dinner home for the family?' the coloured girl working the drive-through had asked him, cheerfully. 'Nope. Just me,' Chops had said with pride, thinking *'mind your fucking business, bitch'*.)

It had been his plan right up until he turned up the volume on the TV as the anchor on Fox had said – '*And the National Rifle Association has just announced that it is posting a reward of half a million dollars for information leading to the arrest of the killer of Bob Beckerman and his associates ...*'

TWENTY-ONE

'Looks like you pushed it a little ...'

Frank was at the golf club at the appointed hour the next day, pulling up the long driveway a little after noon. He let out a whistle as it all spooled out in front of him.

Trump International, West Palm Beach.

His name was down on the visitors list and the security guard waved him on into the parking lot where Brock was already waiting for him. Before he was even out of the car two valets descended on him – one taking his golf bag towards the cart, the other handing him a ticket and parking the car itself, looking at Frank's Camry as though it was a skateboard or a kid's tricycle, here among the Lexuses, the Range Rovers and the Benzes. 'Afternoon, Frank!' Brock said.

'Boy, they take care of you here, don't they?'

'Sure do,' Brock said, putting a tanned arm around him, leading him towards the clubhouse, lowering his voice as he went on, 'Mind you, with these membership fees, right?'

Frank whistled. 'Far cry from old Schilling Country Club ...'

'It sure is, son. Nicer weather in November too, huh? Now come on, we got half an hour or so, we'll grab some coffee, I'll show you the locker room ...'

By the time they were in the cart – the cart itself a kind of mini-limo, with GPS, tinted windshield and an icebox packed with frosty sodas and beers – Frank was stupefied with opulence. Everything, from the thickness of the hand towels (rolled, not folded) to the glassware and flatware, from the carpeting to the complimentary markers, tees and balls you were given, screamed *here is money*. Frank watched as Brock said hello to fellow members, introduced him to some of them, these retired bankers, doctors, dentists and construction magnates, all seeing out their days under the Florida sun, all of them paying the $150,000 joining fee, then another forty-odd thousand a year in dues, all so they could relish the fading of their lives in this glorious place, this fortress of furious solvency, at what they surely saw as the most glorious time in American history – all of them now paying something like 15 per cent in taxes.

'Take it away,' Brock said, gesturing to the first tee – a long par four, with a creek winding all the way along the right-hand side, thick trees and rough in there too. Frank stepped up, lined up the shot and took a few preparatory waggles, before, to no one's surprise more than his own, he striped it 260 yards straight down the middle. 'Hey!' Brock said. 'Easy there, son! You know, maybe you should be giving me a few shots here ...'

They rode through the greenery in the cart. Brock lit up a Cohiba and talked about the club. About how the second tee box was built over the nuclear fallout shelter the original owners had built during the Korean War. About the new tee box they'd put in at 14, adding thirty yards to the hole. About his buddy Van Peters, whose eight-iron at the par three fourteenth had been so close to a hole in one the other week, it had just lipped out. And about the former president. His last visit. His next visit, a couple of weeks from now. About how he could still shoot his age at eighty. (Although questions remained about his sporting conduct, the fact that he routinely gave himself putts that would have troubled a pro, an inability to count penalty strokes, to count past five in fact.) How he worked the patio, the dining room and the course, happy to talk to anyone. About how some of the members would grouse to him about Ivanka, with her touchy-feely policies, her softening up on ICE and the border. Reuniting these goddamned filthy immigrant kids with their parents. It was funny, Frank often thought, take some men of a certain generation away from their wives, put them in the men-only several-hundred-acre green bar room of the golf course, and something happened to them. They felt free to be themselves, or at least a version of themselves they couldn't be at home, in polite company.

Damn gubernmint ... finish the wall ... damn scavengers ... send 'em all back, look after our own ...

After a while, even though he was playing well, just four over par and three holes up in their match play competition, Frank began to feel ill. Not just the daily ill he felt from the cancer washing through his body, from the pills he was taking, no, this was something else. He felt ill from the amount of this type of stuff he'd listened to in a lifetime playing golf on American courses. The type of stuff he himself used to say.

America First ... damn UN ... you look at what Pootin did for his country, they were wiping their asses barehanded ... damn Democrats ... yeah, right, could use some of that global warming ... a holocaust of the unborn is what they want.

It was only when Brock said this last sentence (in relation to the Democrats repeated attempts to reverse the overturning of Roe v Wade – they'd foolishly thought for a moment they might have found an ally in Ivanka), as they drove towards the ninth tee, that Frank nearly spoke up. Nearly told Brock of the story of his only daughter dying in a motel room, having travelled hundreds of miles alone to have an unlicensed abortion. (And what use, the editor in Frank wondered, was that 'unlicensed' these days? All abortions were unlicensed now.) But he just smiled weakly. He still needed Brock. For the last part. The hardest. And here, at the next hole, was where he had to do his thing.

He'd studied the course. The ninth seemed perfect.

From his long hours staring at Google Earth, at the course guides and scorecards he'd printed off the internet, Frank already knew the hole well. A par five, just under five hundred yards, with palm trees and shrubbery along the right-hand side of the fairway. All golfers over a certain level of ability have a shot they can usually hit on demand and for Frank this was a high fade, moving from left to right, a shot that, if he exaggerated it correctly, would whale way off to the right, becoming a push, then a slice. He'd won the last hole ('You're killing me here,' Brock had said) so it was his honour.

Frank set the ball up forward in his stance, opened the club face up a little, and took the driver well outside the line on the takeaway. The slightest pause at the top of his backswing and then he unloaded. Frank watched the ball rocket off, high on a straight line, but then arcing right, farther right and farther right, clattering into the palms, into the bushes. 'Ah shit,' he said.

'Damn,' Brock said, secretly pleased. 'Looks like you pushed it a little ...'

But now, for it to work, Frank needed Brock to find the fairway. As the old man lined up his drive, Frank was more nervous than he had been for some time on a golf course, probably since he sunk that five-foot putt to win the club championship, years ago, when his son was a toddler.

Your wife and your son waiting for you at home. You'd got back to Pippa chopping vegetables for a stew and you'd told them, 'The hell with it, we're going out for a steak dinner!' You hadn't known then that that was as good as life got. That it would never get that good again.

Brock brought the driver back. Frank closed his eyes until he heard the metallic tang of a good connection. He opened them to see his partner not watching his shot, just swiftly and nonchalantly picking up his tee, as amateur golfers did after they knew they'd hit a good drive, because it was what they saw the pros do on TV. The pros only kept a careful eye on the bad drives. But, unlike the pros, most amateurs couldn't help pausing and turning back to enjoy an eyeful of the rare sight of a well-struck bomb tracing straight down the fairway, as Brock did now. 'You caught that one,' Frank said.

'Toed it some,' Brock said bashfully as he got into the cart, Frank already in the driving seat.

'You gonna go for the green?' Frank asked, accelerating down the fairway.

'Mmmm, reckon I've still got nearly 240 from there.'

'Come on, Brock. No guts, no glory.'

Brock laughed. 'What the hell. Long time since I had an eagle putt ...'

'That's the spirit. I'll drop you off at your ball, you take what you need, and I'll drive on up into the scrub and start looking for mine.'

'You sure you don't want a hand?' Brock, already drooling at the prospect of getting a hole back.

'Nah. It went in pretty deep. If I can't find it fast I'll just concede the hole.'

'OK ...'

Brock hopped out – taking his three-wood, his sand wedge and his putter – and Frank accelerated up the shallow hillside into the treeline, out of sight of his playing partner. He jumped out of the cart and looked around – making sure he was fully hidden by the dense foliage. He found a spot between a thick rhododendron bush and the trunk of a palm tree and scrabbled in his golf bag. Frank took out the two items he'd brought.

A ziplocked plastic bag and a trowel.

He dug into the earth next to the palm tree, quickly going down about a foot. From over on the fairway, about seventy or eighty yards to his left, he heard a 'clang' followed by a growled 'goddamnit!' He'd have to work fast. Having hit his shot Brock would be coming to help look for Frank's.

Frank dropped the plastic baggie into the hole and filled it in, smoothing over the earth with his foot then kicking some leaves and palm fronds over it. Using the trowel he scored an 'X' deep into the bark of the palm tree just as he heard twigs breaking underfoot and then Brock, quite close, saying, 'Any luck?'

Frank stepped around the tree, wiping his hands on his pants. 'What the hell happened to you?' Brock asked. Frank looked down, his hands filthy, loose earth on his clothes. 'Oh, I fell getting out the cart back there. How'd you get on?'

'Pulled it into the front-left bunker.'

'Still your hole, I think,' Frank said. 'Can't find mine.'

'Wait,' Brock said, walking off to his right, 'what ball are you playing?'

There it was – sitting right out in the open on the other side of the bushes Frank had been digging in. A decent lie too. 'Titleist 4,' Frank said.

'Here you go,' Brock said, masking his disappointment. 'Shit, son – you're nearly twenty years younger than me and your eyes are worse than mine!'

'Sorry, Brock. Thanks.'

Frank knocked it out onto the fairway with a seven-iron. Then he hit a great three-wood just short of the green: one of those pure connections that travelled high and straight, carrying nearly two hundred yards in the air and then rolling out while his opponent whistled in wonder. It was a shot that gave Frank a genuine ache of sadness that – if things went well – this would surely be the second-last round of golf he would play in his life.

Frank knocked it on the green with his pitching wedge and two-putted for bogey six. Brock took two shots to get out of the bunker and then three-putted for a seven. Despite his drive, Frank won the hole to go five up at the turn. 'Jesus, Brock,' Brock hissed at himself, smacking his ball off the green towards the cart with his putter after he missed the last three-footer.

Two hours later, over Trump steaks and Trump fries in the Trump clubhouse, Brock handed over the twenty-dollar bill and toasted the victor. 'Well played, Frank. I nearly fought my way back into it.'

'You sure did,' Frank said. 'Just ran out of road.'

Truthfully Brock had played a little better on the back nine, but it had still been, as Frank's friend Bill used to say, 'money for jam'. Frank had deliberately missed a couple of short putts to let the guy stay in the match until the sixteenth hole, worried that if he beat him too badly Brock might not have him back. He *had* to have him back. In order to make sure of this Frank was going to have to do the very last thing he felt like doing. He was going to have to talk about the fucking cancer.

Brock gave him an opening as he mopped up the last of his *au jus* with some fries (Frank had managed to eat about half of his, could already feel it sitting like concrete in his guts), when he started talking about a buddy of his who'd just got bad news on some tests. 'Yeah,' Brock said, 'really hit him hard.'

'Brock?' Frank said.

And he told him. It didn't take that long. What was there to say? Brock listened, head inclined, just saying 'Oh Frank' and 'Oh Jeez' and, twice, 'As if you haven't been through enough'.

'Oh well,' Frank said at the end. 'There it is.'

'Did they say, I mean how …?'

'Months. Not years.'

'Oh Jeez.'

'It's OK, Brock. Look – thank you for today. It meant a lot. It's one of the few things that still gives me any pleasure, playing golf.'

'Any time, Frank. Seriously, any time.'

Frank went in for the kill. 'How about a couple of weeks from now? Before I go back? Say, the 14th?'

'The 14th …' Brock said, reaching for his club diary. 'Yeah, I'm free.' A pause. 'Oh.'

'What? No good?' Frank felt his blood, his sick, diseased blood, lurch.

'No, it's just …' Brock lowered his voice. 'We got the big man here that week. They notify members in advance when he's going to be here.' Frank already knew this. 'On account of the extra security and whatnot. We can still play, just need to leave a little more time for everything, especially for guests.'

'Right.'

'Tee times get a little congested too. People know he's here, they like to tee off in groups behind or just ahead of him. Get a chance to watch him. Press the flesh if they can.'

'Right.'

'Nearer the day I'll try and get an idea from the pro about what time he's going out and we can either go earlier or later.'

'Sounds good.'

'Look forward to it, Frank. Gimme a chance to get my money back.'

They clinked glasses and sat in silence for a moment until Brock said, 'Oh Christ, Frank. I'm so sorry.'

TWENTY-TWO

'Just doing what any decent citizen should.'

When you only had one possible lead you followed it. It really was that simple. So here he was, in the aisles of the supermarket, escaping the heat, soaking up the A/C while he sourced provisions: a tub of M&Ms, a six-pack of beer, a big bag of pork rinds, a jar of hot dogs, cigarettes and gum, all nestling in his little cart. Having taken care of the sustenance of the body he was thinking about how to keep his mind active; *Guns & Ammo,* the *Enquirer,* a couple of teeny pop magazines, for the pictures. He was looking at the audiobooks, pondering between the new Grisham and the third volume of Donald Trump Jr's memoirs, *Still Triggering* – when he became aware of the conversation, between a mother and daughter just along from him, by the cereals.

'This one,' the little girl was saying. She was about five.

'No no,' the mother said. She lowered her voice and they had a rapid exchange in Spanish.

Chops slipped the Trump Jr into his cart and shuffled towards them. '*Hola*,' he said to the mother, smiling.

'Hi,' she nodded.

Chops looked down at the little girl, smiling. (The smiling face of Chops, not, he had learned, a sight most people found agreeable.) 'Want everything their own way at that age, don't they?'

The woman gave him a weak grin, trying to get on with her shopping, going to move past him with her cart, tugging the little girl's hand. Chops blocked her path. 'Papers?' he said now, his tone still friendly.

'Excuse me?' The woman looked at him.

'You got papers, lady?'

'What are you talk—' But she was already flustered.

'You know exactly what I'm talking about.' Chops's tone changing now, getting hard. 'You a citizen?'

She took him in – a fearsome sight. In Chops's experience it normally went one of two ways at this point. An actual citizen, even if they were a beaner, would bristle with indignation, tell you to go fuck yourself, maybe even get their phone out and start filming you, figuring they'd get themselves some sympathy from all the libs on social media. A non-citizen would just shut it down, try and walk away. As this woman did now, grabbing her kid's hand and trying to get round him.

'Hey, I'm not kidding here,' Chops said. 'Are you a citizen?' The little girl looking scared now, hiding behind the woman's leg. 'OK, if you wanna play it that way ...' Chops took his cell phone out. He had the number on speed dial: the national hotline. Put you through to your regional office in seconds. He started dialling.

The woman stepped in closer to him. 'Please, mister. Please.' Her eyes were darting, panicked now, all that stony defiance gone in an instant.

'I knew it,' Chops said, sighing. The way she'd lowered her voice when she'd slipped into Spanish.

'You've reached the ICE national hotline. To report an illegal immigrant press 1 now ...'

'No! Please, mister!'

Chops pressing 1.

'Please give your location after the tone ...'

'Uh, I'm at –'

And now the woman made a run for it, grabbing the kid and crashing into a display of cornflakes as she headed for the door. Chops didn't panic. He took his piece out of the small of his back – the little .38 he always carried – and calmly fired a single shot into the ceiling.

'I'm sorry, I didn't understand that. Please ...'

The woman froze, her hands going up even as she got to her knees to comfort the screaming child. A supermarket employee finally appeared.

'What the hell?' the kid began.

Chops held up his badge. 'Police officer. Get the manager. These here are illegals.'

'I'm sorry – I didn't get that. Please give your location after the tone ...'

Chops gave the address and then helped the manager lock the woman and the kid in the storeroom while they waited. The wagon was there within fifteen minutes: four ICE agents in full battledress coming in the store. Perhaps mindful of the small crowd that had gathered now, of the CCTV cameras dotted around the place, they gently and respectfully marched the two illegals to the van. The sergeant in charge turning back to shake Chops's hand. 'Thank you, sir,' he said.

'Hell, just doing what any decent citizen should.'

'Citizen.' It was a sacred word to him. Being a citizen wasn't simply a birthright. It had to be earned. And it had to be earned by every generation, wrenched away from those who would try to dilute it, claimed and reclaimed in blood if necessary.

Exhausted from his efforts, Chops added an ice-cream sandwich to his shopping. He went out and sat on a bench across from the supermarket, overlooking the lake, listening to the jet skis buzzing and watching the heat haze rippling and feeling pretty good as he ate his ice cream and looked around at all the good citizens going about their business. Two fewer grasping mouths, two more snouts removed from the trough of America, Chops thought. He opened the bag of pork rinds.

TWENTY-THREE

**'Sometimes in losing a battle, you find a way
to win the war.'**

Three days later the early afternoon found Frank driving
west across Texas, along the 10, the coast road, the Gulf
of Mexico shining flat and grey on his left, the Bob Dylan
song much on his mind after he'd spent the previous night
in a motel outside Mobile, having driven nine hours straight
up from Florida. '*Oh, Mama ...*'

The last three days had not been pleasant. Perhaps it had
been the rich meals he'd done his best to eat – the lamb
at the Schmidts' place, that steak in the clubhouse – or
perhaps it was a delayed reaction to all that he'd been
through in the previous week or so, what with killing six
people now (officially making him a serial killer, he'd realised with grim satisfaction), or maybe it was just the
progress of the disease. Or a combination of all these
things. Whatever the reason, straight after he got back to
the condo from the golf game, he'd pretty much spent

forty-eight hours in bed, weak as a kitten, only managing to eat a little soup and drink some weak tea. He'd had to punch another hole in his belt. There was one upside to this time: in three days of watching TV he remained unconnected to the killings.

Up ahead, on his right, outside of Corpus Christi, glinting under the Texan sun, he saw it, the first one he'd seen in real life, not just on TV. He pulled over onto the verge and got out the car to look at it, maybe half a mile away, down a long drive. Like many of the others it was a former branch of SupraMart, just off the interstate. The exterior of the huge metal shell was still painted the same drab brown as a regular SupraMart, but there the similarities ended. This one had no signs for special offers in the windows. Had, in fact, no windows at all, all of them having been blacked out. Chain-link fencing topped with razor wire surrounded the place, studded with signs warning 'GOVERNMENT PROPERTY' and 'NO TRESPASSING' and 'ARMED RESPONSE'. In the distance he could see guards patrolling with dogs. The original building had been much extended and modified, with the former parking lot now mostly converted into overspill accommodation – hastily built wooden huts arranged in rows, a guard tower with machine guns and klieg lights at every corner. What was it they called them now? That was it – FRCs: Family Resettlement Centers.

They'd first sprung up back in 2018, during the first term, when they'd started arresting anyone trying to come in illegally. It had meant separating kids from their parents, and the media and the Democrats had gone bananas. Trump had almost abandoned it as a vote loser, especially among

women, but he'd held the line – relentlessly insisting it that
it was Obama who had started it all, who had built these
terrible cages, and that he was just following the law. After
his stunning re-election in 2020 FRCs were one of the first
things they poured money into. New and improved. They
no longer separated families of course, well, they did, but
it had been refined. The new Homeland Security Secretary,
Stephen Miller, had successfully argued that – given the
scale they would now be doing this on, and the increasing
amount of time people were being held for as the deporta-
tions backlog grew – it would be self-defeating to allow
the sexes to mix in the new facilities: human nature being
what it was they would soon be breeding more immigrants
than they were sending back. And of course those new
children wouldn't even technically be immigrants as they
would have been born here, creating further legal night-
mares. So, families were sent to the same camps, but the
women and children under fourteen were housed in one
block and all the men were housed in another. After they
turned fourteen, the boys joined their fathers, uncles,
brothers and cousins in the men's block while the girls
remained with the women.

And what a scale they were doing this on now.

After the trade tariffs had begun to really bite, poverty
– and its associates: drugs and violence – in South America
had gone through the roof. The number of people trying
to cross the border illegally had tripled. So now you had
FRCs all along the southern border. Over a hundred of
them had sprung up in the last few years, stretching from
Brownsville in the east all the way to San Diego in the
west, the average centre housing two thousand detainees,

but the big supercentres, like the one Frank was looking at now, holding perhaps ten to fifteen thousand. (And what a boon it had been to SupraMart, whose ailing retail empire was on its knees after decades of Amazon. Huge government contracts were awarded. Dozens of supermarkets that had been teetering on the brink of collapse were repurposed for detainment.)

The inmates were there for anything from a couple of months to a few years, depending on the complexity of their case and the efficiency of the legal representation they could afford. It was tough to get official figures but it seemed likely that in 2026 at any given time the US was holding around half a million detainees. Inevitably, whole ancillary industries had sprung up around the camps: legal and medical, transportation to and from them, catering contracts, clothing, construction. And then the black markets that cluster anywhere large groups of people are held en masse: prostitution, gangs, drugs and child abuse. You could read articles online (about the only place left where you could find critical accounts of government policy) that detailed the abuses at some of the centres: the governor who was running an on-site brothel, open to locals. The children and babies who simply went missing, sold off to childless couples, or into slavery, or worse. The padded invoices paid to the private contractors who ran the places, often charging close to a thousand dollars a day to house a single inmate, a figure that suggested a five-star hotel, high-thread-count sheets and filet mignon. In reality: a bit of cement floor, foil blankets and bowls of rice. The billions ('*billions and billions of dollars*', Frank could still hear Trump saying in his head) that were getting siphoned off throughout the system, the kickbacks upon kickbacks. Of course, this stuff was all under the counter. Openly, above the counter, a large part of the cost of the centres was offset by the inmates own labours. They were made to work for their bed and board, sewing mailbags and so forth. Doing highway maintenance, cleaning and construction work. In his last months in office Trump had been trying to broker an ambitious synergistic deal whereby future Amazon warehouses would be sited next to the camps, with underground tunnels delivering the free labour straight from the prison to the shop floor: increasing profits for shareholders, slashing prices for consumers, everyone winning. There was even talk of a 'Work to Remain' programme, whereby, after so many years of free labour in the camps, you would have amassed enough credits to be considered for US citizenship. But the deal failed to get concluded before the end of Trump's second term and it had not yet been revived by Ivanka, who, it was said, worried about the optics of profiting from slave labour more than her father had. Frank remembered a recent press trip she'd done, to a facility like one of these. It had obviously had a lot of money pumped into it for her visit and she was variously photographed walking along between neat rows of perfectly made-up bunk beds, beaming with delight at clean, toy-stocked kiddies' play areas, and, in the shot that made most of the front pages, grinning in an apron as she served soup to a smiling throng of children, all of them looking delighted to be meeting the president. It had looked a far cry from what Frank was looking at now. He could see people moving around in the distance, in a yard off to one side of the main building, a dusty square enclosed with razor wire, clearly some kind of exercise yard, containing hunched brown figures, shambling around in a circle.

On impulse he levelled his new iPhone at the huge, jerry-built monstrosity and snapped a photograph. He couldn't read the ironwork sign over the entrance at this distance, but he knew what it said from newspaper articles: 'Sometimes in losing a battle, you find a way to win the war' – a Trump quote. As he slipped his phone back in his pocket his reverie was broken by the sudden yelp of a siren right behind him. He turned around to see a police cruiser pulling up behind his car and two Texas Highway Patrol men getting out.

They strolled towards Frank, their polished brown boots kicking up clouds of dust. 'Excuse me, sir,' the first trooper said, a small guy with a dark moustache, maybe in his early thirties. 'Can I ask what you're doing here?'

'I was just … I hadn't seen one of these before. I'm on vacation.'

'You know taking photographs of government installations is against the law?' The other trooper stood behind the guy, staring at Frank. He was much bigger, over six foot, with a blond buzz cut. Both of them were expressionless behind mirrored Aviators.

'No. I didn't know that. How … how was I supposed to?' Frank gestured around at the empty landscape.

'There's signs up ahead. At the entrance.'

'Well, I didn't know that.'

'Licence and identification,' the little moustache said.

'But why?'

'Excuse me?' Moustache said. Frank saw his name badge now – Daniels.

'Why do you –'

'Listen, buddy,' the blond guy – McAllister according to his badge – said, stepping around his partner, 'break out some ID right now or this is gonna be the worst day of your fucken life.'

Stunned, Frank looked at Daniels as if to say 'what the fuck?' Daniels just spat on the ground.

'Are you threatening me?' Frank asked. 'Because I'm a US taxpayer and I –'

It happened so fast. Trooper McAllister clamped one hand on Frank's left shoulder and with the other grabbed his right arm, twisting it up behind his back as he slammed Frank's face hard down onto the trunk of his own car. The hot metal burned against his cheek. 'What are you doing?' Frank screamed.

'Shut the fuck up, you little pissant,' McAllister hissed.

'Where's the ID, sir?' Daniels asked pleasantly,

'In . . . in my coat. On the passenger seat. You, ow! You're hurting my wrist!' McAllister just ground his face harder into the hot metal. Frank felt something going on behind him and a second later cooler metal against his skin – hand-cuffs going around his wrists.

McAllister stood him up as Daniels came back out of the car with Frank's wallet, hissing, 'You stand right there. Move off this fucken spot and I'll break your fucken nose.'

'Mr Frank Brill,' Daniels said, reading off Frank's licence. 'From Schilling, Indiana.'

'Yes,' Frank said. He felt sick. Weak. His limbs all lique-fied.

'You're a long way from home, Mr Brill. What brings you to Texas?'

'I'm on vacation,' Frank said, struggling to breathe. 'Look, I have a medical condition. I have cancer.'

'Get his phone, Greg.'

McAllister patted Frank's pockets – Frank handcuffed, powerless – and took out Frank's phone, the one he'd bought in Fairfax, his original phone currently the property of the Washington police department. McAllister tossed it to his partner. 'I'm going to need the passwords for your social media accounts, Mr Brill.'

This again. 'I don't have any!'

'Listen, you fuck –' McAllister stepped towards him.

'Easy, Greg,' Daniels said, stopping the bigger man. Daniels sighed, took his sunglasses off and looked at Frank. Being able to see his eyes revealed no humanity. 'Sir, we have reason to suspect that you may have been taking photographs of this facility with a view to posting them on social media in order to create a derogatory narrative.'

It took Frank a moment to take all this in. 'And so what if I was?'

'That's illegal, sir. Under the terms of the –'

'Let me guess,' Frank interrupted. 'Extreme Patriot Act?'

Daniels smiled. 'So you have heard of the law. Now, unless you want to spend the next seventy-two hours in a jail cell, I suggest you start cooperating.'

It was hot, the Texan sun strobing above them, the heat haze rippling up off the road. Frank's legs were getting weak, getting heavier as the fight fuel burned out of them. 'I promise you – I don't have any social media accounts.'

Frank stood there as he went through it. Daniels checked all the apps, not that Frank had many, to make sure he wasn't lying, and then said, 'I'm not going to confiscate your phone. Even though we have the right to do so. I'm just going to delete the photos you took here.'

'You can do that?'

'Yes, sir,' Daniels said, finishing, tucking the device back into Frank's pocket. 'Now, I suggest you get back in your car and get on the road to wherever you're going. There's nothing that concerns you here.' He gestured to the building behind them.

Frank thought about saying, 'As a US taxpayer I've funded that building. Why can't I photograph it?' He thought about saying, 'I've got both of your names and I'll be reporting you for police brutality.' He thought about saying, 'Fuck you.' He thought about saying a lot of stuff. But then he looked around him, at the vast expanse of Texas, at the empty highway, at the total absence of CCTV cameras. There would be no footage of him getting beaten up. No clip or GIF to go viral. He thought about all this and he didn't say anything. Just took his licence back and started getting into his car. 'You have a good day now,' McAllister said as he closed the door behind him.

Frank sat there, watching the cruiser accelerate into the distance, watching it vanish into the rippling heat. He felt shaken, certainly. Violated. But he found he wasn't amazed, *staggered* by the experience, as he certainly would have been twenty – even ten – years ago if a police officer in his own country had, for the second time in a week, insisted on having access to his private messages. It did, as they say, happen inch by inch, day by day, until you woke up one morning and found yourself in a place where the unthinkable had become very thinkable, had then become doable and had finally become routine. *Shit, now I do it just to watch their expressions change.*

He was a couple of miles down the road before the one piece of good fortune dawned on him – they hadn't bothered to run his plates.

He got to San Antonio later that day, checked into a motel, found his way to the exclusive suburb of Champions Ridge, and began the usual surveillance.

TWENTY-FOUR

'Think of all the lives we've saved.'

'Jesus Christ, this fucking guy.' 'Debbie' fixed her stocking tops, checking her make-up in the mirror. 'Every Tuesday . . .'

'It's not too bad – hell, he can't even get it up no more.' This was 'Kelly', making adjustments to her outfit, both girls cramped in the milky plastic light of the bathroom. This was another thing, all the money this guy had, you'd think he could spring for a decent hotel. But no, it was always the same, every Tuesday afternoon, this cheap Motel 6 off the interstate. Debbie – twenty now, but going out as nineteen on the website – had been here many times. Kelly was seventeen, but going out as eighteen of course. This was her third visit. Both of the girls were standard for the agency: blonde hair, big fake tits, and hard, tanned, perfect bodies. They both came from small Texan towns, were both saving up to move to LA, and were both wearing the standard accoutrements of the business – thongs, stockings, belly chains. Additionally, Kelly was wearing a large, black strap-on dildo.

'Hurry it up in there now. Papa Bear's waiting!' His voice came through from the bedroom, gruff and wattled, the voice of a man used to shouting at waiters.

'Shit, darling,' Debbie whispered to Kelly, 'that's easy for you to say. Least you get to be the guy.' She eyed the black rubber phallus buckled to her colleague's waist.

'You wanna swap?' Kelly asked, but with little conviction.

'Hell, it's OK.' They'd only worked together a few times, but a protective, older-sister dynamic had already developed. 'Just make sure you get plenty of this shit on it.' She handed her the KY.

'DAMN IT – COME ON NOW!'

They came out of the bathroom, Debbie first, sashaying forward onto the bed. Kelly came out behind her, placed her hands on her hips and cocked a leg to the side to best display the enormous black monster, wanging lazily in front of her, the leather of the straps already cutting into her flesh.

The man clapped delightedly. He was sitting in a tub chair in his tighty-whities, drinking bourbon from a plastic cup. 'Now that's what ah'm talking about. God damn.'

'What do you want today, lover boy?' This was Debbie on the bed, already, automatically, playing with herself.

'Looks like a black cock, don't it?' the guy said. 'Like a big old hunk of dark meat.' The girls giggled. 'You like that black cock, darling?' He asked this directly to Kelly, knowing she was younger, more insecure. Kelly was unsure of the right answer here. A 'no' might turn him off, but a 'yes' might enrage him.

'Not as much as I like yours, Papa Bear,' she cooed, all the while running a hand up and down the dildo she was wearing. He looked at it, his hand inside his shorts, playing with himself. Debbie watched his cruel, calculating face, his Adam's apple bobbing up and down once, quickly, as he stared at Kelly and swallowed back his lust. Debbie thought back to her Bible classes in Denton. Adam, the first man, the one who'd spawned all these fucks they had to deal with every day. Debbie also noticed he wasn't staring at Kelly so much as he was staring at the fucking dildo. Figured. Half queer lots of these fellas anyway. Probably been dreaming of a black guy's cock inside him all his life. 'What do I want you to do?' The old guy – old enough to be their grandpa, their *great*-grandpa – repeated it with a half-incredulous tone. He took a long draught of bourbon and smacked his lips. 'I want you –' he pointed to Kelly – 'to stick that big nigger dick up her ass –' his finger moving to point at Debbie. 'You pound it hard now.' Both the girls were too young to remember this man's time on the centre stage of American politics. If they had they would have been stunned at the gulf between the public and the private image.

'Oh *goody*,' Debbie said with as much enthusiasm as she could manage, getting up onto her knees on the bed, pushing her ass towards Kelly. A long strand of jelly dripped from the monstrous toy, glistening in the afternoon sunlight that streamed through the thin, closed curtains.

Kelly moved into position, pressing the tip against Debbie's bottom. Debbie gasped at the cold of it. 'Slowly now,' the man said, sitting up in the chair, moving his bulk forward to get a better look.

Debbie braced herself.

There were three staccato knocks at the door.

'Police. Open up.'

All three participants froze. Kelly and Debbie looked at the man. The man looked at the door. A beat and then three more knocks. Harder.

'San Antonio PD. Open the door, sir.'

What the fuck? The man got unsteadily to his feet, the minute semblance of an erection he had managed to attain fast disappearing. With his left hand he held an angry finger to his lips and with his right he pointed to the bathroom door. The girls quickly scrambled towards it and closed the door behind them. 'Just a damn minute,' the man said gruffly, pulling his pants on, sweating, breathing hard with the effort, thinking – *whoever the fuck this is I'll have their fucken badge*. He opened the door. A man was standing there. Maybe in his sixties. Grey hair spilling out from under a black woollen cap or beanie.

'Mr Rockman?' the guy said.

Before Rockman could answer he was reeling backwards, clutching his nose as blood spurted out of it, crashing onto the bed.

Frank stepped into the room, locking the door behind him and pointing the .38 snub nose he'd just used to break Rockman's nose straight at the cowering octogenarian.

'Who the fuck are you?' Rockman yelled from the floor.

'I'll be Frank,' Frank said. He had to admit it, he was kind of into it now.

He'd been watching him for over a week now, following the ancient retiree around San Antonio. From his mansion in the affluent suburb, to his golf course, to the deli he favoured, to this motel, the target was a creature of habit. He had visited here last Tuesday afternoon, at exactly the same time, parking far away from the room and strolling over, then opening the door about a half-hour later to two young women dressed in jogging clothes, but both carrying holdalls. It seemed that the many rumours about Rockman – with his eight children from four different wives – were true. He had his appetites, although indulging those appetites did not seem to have put any kind of dampener on his enthusiasm for inflicting a much more heavy-handed, biblical view of morality upon the people of America. Frank had felt strongly that the following Tuesday Rockman would be repeating his motel routine and, if he did, Frank would be ready with the .38 he'd acquired in a pawn store on the outskirts of town.

'What ... what ...' Rockman was in shock, flailing backwards, tumbling onto the floor, suddenly looking very old and feeble.

Frank stepped around him and pulled down his beanie, actually a woollen ski mask, obscuring his face except for the eye and mouth holes. He tapped on the bathroom door with the butt of the gun. He looked like a central casting rapist.

'Girls? Open the door. Come on now. You're not in any trouble and no one's going to hurt you.'

A moment and then Debbie opened the door, Kelly behind her on the edge of the tub. 'Oh my God,' Debbie said. Kelly started crying when she saw the mask, his eyes, the gun.

'Shhh,' Frank said. 'Now listen. I'm just going to talk to him for a minute. Two or three minutes tops. Just lock the door and stay –' Behind him he heard a lamp falling over: Rockman, trying to get to his feet, clutching a bedside table. Frank stepped over and kicked him in the ribs, but not too hard, putting him down, whimpering. He turned back to the bathroom. 'Stay in there. OK? This is between me and him. Nothing to do with you.'

Debbie nodded, blinking back tears.

'After I'm gone you girls give me five minutes and then do whatever you have to do.' He looked over at the table where Rockman had been sitting: bourbon, ice bucket, car keys and stuff. Frank went over and picked up Rockman's wallet. It was stuffed thick with cash. 'Here,' Frank said, handing the girl all of it. 'You should have this.' Debbie took the money in shaking hands. 'You don't have any cell phones or anything in there, do you?' Debbie shook her head. 'OK. Shut the door and don't come out. You hear me?'

'How ... how will we know when you're gone?' Debbie asked.

'You'll know. Now stay in there.'

As he went to close the door, Kelly said, 'M-mister?' Frank looked at her over Debbie's shoulder. She was shaking, her face slick with tears, wearing a rubber cock. 'What did he do to you?'

Frank thought for a second. 'He killed my daughter.'

He shut the door, heard it lock from inside.

Frank took the ski mask off and stepped back over towards where Dennis Rockman, former Supreme Court Justice of the United States, was pushing himself feebly back towards the bed, using his bare heels in the carpet, his vest covered with blood from his busted nose. Frank saw he'd lost a front tooth when he'd popped him in the face with the butt of the gun. (This was another thing the movies lied to you about, Frank was discovering. In the movies people got pistol-whipped all the time and they just kind of took it. Maybe there would be a little cut. In real life? You smack someone in the face with a two-pound piece of metal? It really fucks them up.) The broken nose and the missing tooth meant that Rockman's voice was coming out strange, nasal and sibilant, flat with the odd whistle in there. 'Wayy, wayy, wayy jusss a secon,' he was saying, holding up a hand, blood bubbling out the nose, dribbling out the mouth.

Frank sat down in the chair opposite the foot of the bed, Rockman on the carpet, back against the bed. He rested the gun on his thigh, the barrel vaguely pointed at Rockman's chest.

'You gaw th' ron guy. I nebber kill anyone.'

'Five years ago,' Frank began. He was conscious of the fact that he was so much calmer than he'd been with Hauser, than with the dentist. *That first one is the bitch of the bunch.* 'You were appointed to the Supreme Court, where you provided the decisive vote in overturning Roe v Wade. That led to a nationwide abortion ban. A couple of years later, my daughter died from complications arising from a badly performed illegal abortion.' Frank let this sink in. Rockman's face showed confusion, then panic.

'I'm sorry, I'm sorry for your loss but ... but ... it's not my fault.'

'Whose fault is it?'

Rockman looked at him, at the slightly trembling gun clamped in his fist, the experienced prosecutor inside him feeling around for the magic word or phrase the judge wanted to hear, the one that would get him out of this. 'Well, I was just one voice on the court. Yes, yes I did vote to overturn that particular statute. I voted with my *conscience*.'

Frank cocked the gun.

'No! No! Wait! You want money? I have lots of money.'

'That's not going to help you here.'

Rockman saw that it wasn't. Tried a different tack. 'Son, I'm a retired Supreme Court Justice. Think. Come on – use your damn head! You kill me, your life's over. They're going to get you and you'll go to the chair.'

'My life's already over. I have cancer.'

Oh shit. Rockman scratching around now, desperate, looking for an angle. 'Look, we ... we believe in different things. You say I caused your daughter's death. But, look at it from my point of view. Think ... think of all the babies. Think of all the lives we've *saved*.'

'What about my daughter? My little girl, bleeding to death in her sleep in some room like this. All on her own. I think about it all the time, you know? Did she wake up at some point? Did she know what was happening to her? Was she scared? All alone. Maybe crying out for her mommy. Or ...' Here Frank's voice broke. He sucked it back in through his teeth. '... for her daddy.'

Silence for a moment, just the rasp of breathing in through the blood bubbles in his nose, Frank tapping the cocked revolver against his thigh. And then in a new tone, the placatory, reasonable tone he had used in many court-rooms, way back when he was a prosecutor trying to get a tough judge onside, Rockman began, 'You know, Frank, in the Bible it says –'

'The Bible?' Frank said. 'The *Bible*? Oh, that's good. That's great. Tell me, Justice Rockman, what does it say in the Bible about jerking off to teenage hookers wearing dildos? Was that in the Old or the New Testament? I must have missed that passage.'

Rockman met Frank's gaze and found some strength within himself, dredging it up through his pain and his fear. 'I'm not perfect, sir. I am a sinner. I will have to meet the Lord on even terms. I will confess and, God willing, have my sins absolved. Praise Jesus. And I am sorry for your loss. Truly. But what I did in my life will count against what happened here today. I helped to stop a holocaust of a generation of unborn innocents. Think of that now. If you believe all lives to be equal I have done more good than harm.'

He managed to get all of this out with a kind of dignity, a proud defiance, even as he sat there in blood-soaked vest and underpants, with his face and teeth all busted up and two hookers cowering in his bathroom. Yes, no doubt about it, you could feel the smarm and charm oozing, could see why this tough old son of a bitch would have made a difficult, dangerous opponent back in the day.

Frank pressed a pillow to his face, put the gun to it to muffle the shot, and pulled the trigger.

He heard the screams and sobs from the bathroom, but he'd closed his eyes so he didn't see the shovelful of blood and brains that was blasted up the bedspread and across the cheap wood panelling. He threw the gun in the trash can and walked out the door, taking his gloves off and pulling the beanie down over his forehead, covering as much of his face as he could.

There was no one in the parking lot. Frank crossed the street and made a right down an alleyway. In less than five minutes he was in his car and back on the interstate, heading south, heading back towards the Sunshine State.

TWENTY-FIVE

'Most of the debits are to do with love.'

'I think it's terrible. I think it's a disgrace.'

Frank turned up the volume on the TV.

'You see now, with the crime. Because we've got to get even tougher. And ... he was a good man. I put him in there, you know that, right? I made that decision and then he, he made a great, a tremendous decision, a decision for this country that saved, well, who knows how many lives. Think of it – in the last five years, let alone the future. They say there were half a million, maybe more, maybe a lot more, but they say half a million babies were being murdered, in the womb, in this country, because the Democrats – and the Republicans too, you got to say that – they'd allowed it for so long. And I stopped it. And Judge Rockman played a part in that. A big part. So you got to give him credit. So it's a terrible way for a great life to end, but I think history will remember him as a great, a tremendous conservative and a great thing, really, for this country.' The wind whipped across the runway, the helicopter powering up in the background, sending the former president's candyfloss wispy hair swirling around. The moment he stopped talking the reporters started shouting, like they'd been doing for more than a decade now.

'Mr Trump!'

'Sir!'

'Former President Trump!' one tried, going for respect, hoping to be picked. But Trump pointed at another guy.

'Sir, what do you say to the allegations that former Justice Rockman was with two prostitutes when he died?'

'I'm not going to comment on that. No, I'm not going to comment because these are just ... sick rumours. Probably started by the left. Who knows, but probably. What I will say is that from what I know of Dennis Rockman – good Christian, good family man – I wouldn't be surprised if these turn out to be just another sick, fake news attempt to smear a great man's reputation. Because you saw, you remember, no, excuse me, you saw when we overturned Roe v Wade. They said, "Oooh, you'll never overturn Roe v Wade. Too tough." You know what – I got it done. They said, they still say, maybe no one else could have got it done. And the liberals and the Democrats and the fake news, all you guys went crazy. He, Justice Rockman, he got death threats, just the worst kind of things. Things you wouldn't believe. The hatred. Sick. And so he was brave, a brave man to do it. As I was, by the way. I need to give myself some credit there because you guys never will. And I delivered on what I promised the American people. Unlike all the other presidents – except Ivanka, right? She's doing great, isn't she? I know some people say, "Ooh, she's not as tough as her old man was," but you know what? Give her a break. She's learning. She's learning. And you know what? It's a steep curve, let me tell you. It's – the things you've got to be on top of as president? No one knows. No one knows how tough it is, But, unlike all the others, I did what I said I was gonna do. More than any administration in history I think. But the point is, these rumours, I'd say to anyone printing them, anyone broadcasting them, be careful. Be very, very careful. Because, as you know, we toughened up the libel laws before I left office. We made it a lot harder for you guys –' Trump pointed at the assembled press – 'to just go and say whatever you want. So I think, right now, we focus on catching the killer, bringing him, or her, could be a her, who knows? Because the women, back when we made that decision, the women, some of them went a little crazy, right? So it could be a woman. But I think what's important is that we focus on catching the killer and not on discussing these sick, fake news rumours. OK? Thanks, guys. Bye-bye. I'm heading down to Mar-a-Lago now, the winter White House we called it when I was president, I guess Ivanka still does. We're looking forward to a great, a truly great season there. We're fully booked all winter at Palm Beach, just solid. But if –' he turned towards the nearest camera – 'if you want the Trump winter experience, there's Trump Miami Beach, which I just opened last year and it really is, just a tremendous, tremendous resort. OK. Thanks.'

A phalanx (another word never used anywhere but in the written context, the editor would have reflected) of Secret Service agents engulfed the hulking black shape and started leading him towards the helicopter. The CNN anchor's face filled the screen. 'And that was former President Trump, at Andrews Air Force Base earlier this morning, commenting on the news from Texas of the murder of former Supreme Court Justice Dennis Rockman. And the current president had this to say ...' Frank turned the sound down as it cut to Ivanka talking in the Rose Garden. He'd seen the clip already this morning.

He yawned and stretched out on the huge bed in the New Orleans Four Seasons. Maybe it was the aftertaste of Rockman, that terrible squalid motel, whatever the reason, last night, having driven ten hours south and east, Frank couldn't face the usual set of cinder-block rooms off the highway, with the drained pool and the broken waterbeds and the locked phones in the rooms. He'd wanted to spend just one night in a nice hotel. So he'd taken the exit for New Orleans and checked in here, paying over seven hundred dollars for a deluxe room.

He sipped his coffee and looked out the window at the city, starting to come to life many floors below him, and thought about the last few weeks. Oklahoma, Vegas, Washington, Florida, Texas, now New Orleans ... thousands of miles. He'd seen so much of the country and – so far – had gotten away with seven homicides in four states. Had he expected it to be more difficult? He'd been pretty sure he could get away with Hauser and Roberts, but the others ...

Then again, there were some factors helping him.

There had been a record-breaking 29,456 firearm-related homicides in the USA in 2025, including forty-two mass shootings. Against this backdrop Frank's little old seven-killings-in-four-different-states looked like what it was – a few random acts of completely normal, garden-variety violence. Also helping him, he reflected, sprawling there in the enormous bed high above the Big Easy, was the fact that law enforcement had been gutted on both local and national levels over the course of the last ten years. The FBI was a shell of its former self, half its field agents gone. The only law enforcement agency who had seen an upside to a decade of Trumpism was, of course, ICE, whose budgets had soared.

Meanwhile, in all the major conurbations, crime was up and police departments were struggling, stretched taut as razor wire. Interestingly, the public perception was still that the Republicans were the party of law and order and that, given the chance again after ten years in the wilderness, the Democrats would usher in an apocalypse, a carnival of crime. Why did people think this? Well, because, and despite all statistics to the contrary, the administration just kept saying it. Frank looked at the newspapers spread out on the bed – the *Washington Post*, the *New York Times*, the *New Orleans Sentinel* – and counted seven different stories where leading members of the cabinet (Miller, Conway, Hannity and Gorka) trumpeted, without correction, misleading claims about crime statistics and Democrat policies. The few crime stories that were reported all focused on crimes by illegal immigrants. (Since the Freedom of the Press Act 2022, the act Trump had been referring to on the TV a moment ago, all of these papers were just state mouthpieces.) In a way, if you were white and American, the new climate was almost an open licence to commit crime.

But couldn't people just look out their windows and see the truth? Not really. The ones who had benefited in recent years, the ones who had seen their tax bills halved, lived in gated communities, in private estates with private security forces they paid for themselves. Most of the bottom half of the population – the ones who lived with all the shootings and the rapes and the muggings and the burglary and the arson – genuinely believed that the government was trying to help them and would be able to do so just as soon as they got rid of all the law-breaking immigrants. Thinking about this, feeling that twitch and burrow in his lower bowels (that second cup of coffee definitely a bad idea) as whatever was killing him worked its way up there, Frank reflected again on how he was glad his time was almost up, that he wouldn't be around to see where things went from here.

He looked back at the TV screen, where they had returned to Andrews, the helicopter, powering up, preparing to take off. Along the bottom of the screen, on the rolling news ticker, Frank saw the words 'NRA INCREASES REWARD FOR BECKERMAN KILLER TO ONE MILLION DOLLARS'. He felt a strange rush of pride as he looked back at the helicopter containing the former president, taking off now, spiralling up into the cold Virginian air, where it hovered for a moment before its black nose dipped, like a beast scenting something, and it headed due south, seeking the sun, the warmth of Florida.

Frank checked out, and, in humbler fashion, did exactly the same thing.

The last leg of the journey, the drive from New Orleans back to Florida, the last long drive he would ever undertake, should have taken nine or ten hours but wound up taking fifteen. There were ICE roadblocks all along the coastal highway, where they were stopping traffic, checking documents, doing all the usual things. Since the US/Mexico land border had become a far harder crossing proposition, many refugees tried coming across the Gulf. They made the trip from the beaches of north-eastern Mexico, striking out in tiny boats, canoes, inflatables even, many dying, the lucky ones landing on the Texan coastline. At one of the roadblocks, just west of Pensacola, Frank saw a dark-skinned man arguing with the officers as they went to lead his friend away from his wife and children. One of the officers shoved the guy back towards his car. The guy shoved the officer back. Down he went in a flurry of billy clubs as four agents descended on him. Many people in the long line of cars got out to watch, some shouting 'STOP! and 'LEAVE HIM ALONE!', others, many more, shouting 'KICK HIS ASS!' and, inevitably, 'USA! USA!' It only took a few seconds until the guy stopped moving, stopped twitching, and was carried – unconscious? dead? – to the wagon. Kids dangled their arms out of the windows of cars, filming the whole thing on their phones, their expressions dispassionate, uninterested. (And how, Frank wondered, will *their* kids feel about all this, twenty years, thirty years from now?) Already two officers were going down the traffic line confiscating phones, reciting the Extreme Patriot Act, words Frank was so familiar with now. They wouldn't get all the phones of course and footage of the attack would show up in the usual places, to support the usual agendas. On CNN as an unprovoked attack on an innocent man, an indictment of the now nearly unlimited powers of ICE. On Fox as brave soldiers defending our freedom, responding to provocation by an illegal immigrant, most likely a member of the dreaded MS-13. On left-leaning websites as proof of a police state. On right-wing ones as proof of state vigilance. The left would believe what they were going to believe and the right would believe what they were going to believe and the people in the middle, the people caught in the churn, would throw their hands up and say – 'How can you know anything any more?'

Frank Brill used to edit a newspaper.

He was glad he would soon be dead.

TWENTY-SIX

'It's gonna sting some …'

It was just after five o'clock the following morning – still pitch-dark – when Frank walked into the condo, exhausted, shaky and drained. Having eaten nothing on the last ten-hour stretch of the drive, he was clutching a paper McDonald's bag containing two sausage-egg McMuffins and four hash browns, the only food he'd been able to get in town at this hour. He dropped his car keys in the fruit bowl by the door and reached for the lamp on the table next to it. Just as he reached the switch he smelled something, something fetid and ripe, booze and nicotine, as though someone had been having a party. He turned the lamp on.

'Good morning,' a voice said.

Frank screamed.

The man was sitting in the lounger by the window. He was big, really fat, and he was pointing a gun straight at

Frank, a big, nickel-plated revolver of some kind. 'Just sit down over there on the sofa, nice and easy,' Chops said. 'Keep holding on to that bag. Hands where I can see 'em.'

The room had been ... destroyed.

All across the floor, on every available surface, there were fast-food cartons, bags of potato chips, beer cans, soft-drink cans, overflowing ashtrays.

Frank almost collapsed onto the sofa, his legs giving out from under him with shock.

'I have money. In the safe,' he croaked.

Chops looked at him, cocking his head a little to the left. 'Sorry about the mess,' he said. 'I been here over a week. Ain't really had time to prioritise the housekeeping, Frank.'

Frank waited.

'I don't want your money, Frank Brill,' Chops went on. 'Well, I'm going to get some money, but not yours.'

'What ... what ...'

'You killed my buddy, back in Oklahoma City. Coach Hauser. I been on your ass for weeks. Don't you fucking lie to me now, or I swear to God –'

'Yes,' Frank said. 'I killed him.'

'Good. We're establishing trust here, Frank.' Chops sat forward, still not taking the gun off Frank. He had a few beers lined up in front of him on the coffee table and he popped one open, slurped. 'And you killed them two faggots? Over in Vegas?'

'Yes.'

'And then Beckerman and those two fellas outside of DC?'

'Yes.'

'That was a bold one, Frank. And I'm guessing that this very morning –' he pointed at the TV with the snub barrel of the gun – 'you just came back from Texas having killed poor old Justice Rockman.'

Frank didn't say anything.

'See, the first couple, Oklahoma and Vegas, I figured them out myself. Good old-fashioned police work. On Beckerman, I had some help …' Chops held up one of Frank's files, the heavy manila folder. 'These old files gonna go a long way to helping me prove who you are. And, I gotta say, Frank,' Chops laughed, 'number 5 on this list? You got some brass fucking balls, my friend. Hell, I was almost thinking about letting you go just to see how the fuck you was gonna pull that one off.'

'You're a policeman?'

'At first I just wanted to catch the motherfucker who killed my friend. But then, well, you got interesting. Like a million dollars kind of interesting. I was just going to kill you when I found you, get you to confess and then shoot you in the head. But seeing as they're going to fry you anyway, I figured – why not take you in? Then I get paid *and* I can come watch you wriggle in the 'lectric chair.' Chops smiled. A terrible sight.

So this was how it ended, Frank thought. In the old days, the days of due process, he could probably have counted on dying in prison, the cancer doing its work long before he got to trial. Nowadays? With the Accelerated Justice Program? Oh well, he wouldn't be facing the electric chair. Frank knew that. He tensed his legs. Any moment now he was going to lunge. Just attack this guy and – bingo – Death by Cop.

'Now, Frank, don't do anything stupid like trying to come at me and make me kill you.' It was like the man was reading his mind. 'I'll just pop a couple in your legs and then you'll be in agony for a while and then have to be on death row in a wheelchair.' Frank eased back into the sofa. 'There's one thing.' Chops reached into his pocket and took out a small, black plastic device. 'I got to know, what's the link with Roberts in Vegas, Frank? I'm guessing it had to do with your ex-wife? Marty, I get. He was fucking some young buddy of yours back in the day, right?'

'He raped my friend when he was just a kid.'

'Hell.' Chops waved his gun airily. 'You got all worked up to kill a good man over that? Like we say back in Oklahoma, Frank – 'old enough to pull 'em up, old enough to pull 'em down.'

He laughed at Frank's set jaw, at his anger.

'He killed himself,' Frank said.

'Yeah, like twenty years later?' Chops said. 'Lotta shit coulda happened since then. River of cum coulda gone up that boy since then.'

Frank clenched his fists.

'Easy there, tiger,' Chops said. 'Don't do nothing stupid. See, with the NRA guys and Rockman, and the big enchilada on your list here –' he tapped the folder – 'I'd have said you were some crazy libtard. Some left-winger looking to make a statement. But how do them faggots fit into that? Liberals ain't going round killing no homos.'

'Roberts ruined my ex-wi—' Frank began.

'Hold on there. I'm gonna need to record your confession here,' Chops said, turning on the Dictaphone he'd brought out. 'Might need it to back up this folder. Let's hear the whole thing, start to finish.'

'Can I have a glass of water please?' Frank asked.

'Nope, I ain't getting up. But here …' Chops tossed a beer onto the sofa next to Frank.

'I can't drink this.'

'How's that?'

'I'm an alcoholic. I can't drink beer.'

Chops gave a throaty chuckle, shaking his head. 'Hell, son, you just get that beer down you. I wouldn't be worrying too much about that "I'm an alcoholic" bullshit now. You're gonna be dead soon enough.' Frank sighed and set the beer down on the floor. 'Besides,' Chops went on, 'there's too much of this –' he assumed a whiny liberal voice – '"*I'm an alcoholic, I don't eat meat.*" We're fucken Americans. We drink beer and eat cheeseburgers and if you don't like it get the fuck out.'

Frank went to set the McDonald's bag on the carpet. 'Hey,' Chops said. 'What you got in there?'

'McMuffins. Hash browns.'

'Well, shit, hand that fucken bag over.'

'Look, whoever you are –'

'Call me Chops.'

'Chops. I haven't eaten since –'

'Tough titties, pal, I been sitting in this chair for days and you only got basic cable and jackshit in the icebox, so just gimme the fucking food.'

Frank handed over the paper bag. Chops stuffed a hash brown in his mouth. 'Mmmmm. Right, confession. Go.'

Frank began. He talked about his cancer. About Hauser the rapist. About the dentist destroying his ex-wife. About his wife and son dying. About his daughter dying. About all the men he blamed for this stuff. It didn't really take very long. Maybe twenty minutes. Chops nodded and ate one-handed, never taking the gun away, occasionally emitting a bark of laughter, or a snort of disgust, or a brief comment like 'liberal faggot' when Frank talked about the school shooting or about the overturning of Roe v Wade. Chops was munching his way through the second McMuffin when Frank finished talking. 'That it?' he said. Frank nodded. 'OK then.' Chops turned off the recorder and stood up. 'Now listen, son, I don't want you giving me any trouble on the way in. And I figure I owe you some payback for shooting my buddy all up the way you did. So I'm going to kneecap you with this here .38 ...' He held the gun up, showing it to Frank.

'No, please ...'

Chops stuffed the last huge bite of the breakfast sandwich into his mouth and spoke on with difficulty, chewing his way around it. 'Now it's gonna sting some, so you best prepare yourself. OK?'

He levelled the pistol, pulled back the hammer.

'STOP! I WON'T RUN. You don't need to –'

'Ready?'

Chops swallowed. And then his eyes widened as his hands flew to his chest. 'GNNNUUFF!' he said. 'UNNNGH!'

It felt like his heart had contracted, had suddenly clenched into a tight fist inside him.

Oh God, no. Not now, Chops just had time to think.

Frank, shaking, watching, as Chops collapsed to his knees. He was spluttering, gasping for air, his eyes bulging now. He looked at Frank in desperation. Frank stood up. Chops dropped the gun, really panicking now, as he fell onto his back, his knees going up as far as his great belly would allow.

Frank quickly kicked the gun away, sending it clattering across the hardwood floor, as Chops writhed at his feet, turning an alarming shade of purple now. He tried to get up, couldn't. Must have weighed nearly 300 pounds. He fell back down, face into the rug, clawing, kicking his feet. Frank crossed the room, picking up the gun as he went, and watching, grimly fascinated, as Chops beat his fists on the hardwood floor, making a lot of noise, straining, grunting and banging, as the heart attack screamed through him. Frank reached over and turned the stereo on, getting an Orlando station on the FM, turning the volume up. It was getting light outside, dawn just rising over the lake as his would-be killer fought for dear life on the floor.

Chops rolled over onto his back again, was going blue in the face now. Frank had always thought it was just an expression, a piece of hyperbole meant to express frustration or rage, but here it was – the guy's huge, sweating face was pulsating, turning the colour of blueberry juice. Finally, with a schlucking, popping sound comparable to the noise a rubber plunger will make when torn off a blocked plughole, a chunk of half-masticated meat, cheese and bread flew out of Chops's gullet, shooting several feet straight up in the air and falling back down to land on his chest. Frank watched, horrified and compelled. But even with his airway cleared Chops continued gasping for breath as he clutched with both hands at the left-hand side of his chest (his flattened palms, Frank noticed, horribly mashing the regurgitated piece of burger into the front of his plaid shirt), as he kicked his heels against the floor, screeching in agony as the terrible event boiled through him.

It felt to Chops as if his heart had been wrapped in barbed wire, wire that someone was tightening and tightening. 'P-p-p-' he stuttered, trying to find the words to beg Frank for help. But no words were coming.

Frank looked down at Chops, the two sixty-something men making direct eye contact, Chops's eyes wide, panicked, begging, Frank's narrowed, revolted. He brought the gun up. It would be a mercy killing really. The flesh around the guy's mouth was starting to turn black as Frank pulled back the hammer on the revolver. Chops was silent now, in too much pain to make any sound.

'Ah, fuck it,' Frank said, lowering the hammer again.

He stuck the pistol into his belt, turned and walked out of the room and down the hallway, grabbing his bag and his car keys, heading on out of the apartment.

Chops stared hopelessly at the ceiling, everything getting dark now as his vision started to dim and he began to see himself entering the kingdom of heaven. The light he was moving into more golden than white, warm and forgiving, like sunshine, and in it he felt all his sins being absolved, he felt the Lord's forgiveness bathing over him. For the Lord did not care about the petty foolishness Chops had sometimes indulged himself in. What did a few boys matter? He had done so much good, stopped so much evil.

He saw himself ascending towards God, God's hair flying celestially from beneath the red cap, the face of God looking very familiar and Chops feeling no surprise, only confirmation of what he had always believed, that the Lord had indeed made The Chosen One in his own image ...

TWENTY-SEVEN

'Enjoy!'

Frank Brill, on his last night on earth, alone out on the patio, the December evening being too cool for the Floridians, who were all inside, snug behind the thick plate glass. Astonished that his appetite seemed to have returned, but still aware of the events of that morning – and the fact that he was overlooking the Atlantic – he had eschewed red meat (again, a word never used verbally, the editor reflected) and went with seafood all the way: having ordered and demolished a dozen oysters, he was now waiting for the stuffed, baked sea bream.

He had wondered during the course of the day, the return of his appetite . . . could they be wrong? Maybe it had gone away? Maybe the diagnosis was wrong? Should he have sought a second opinion? Would that be the sick, final twist? Had he done all of this, taken all these lives (at least one of them an innocent life), only to not be dying after all? It didn't much matter any more. Talking of things that didn't matter any more, he realised he'd been staring at the wine list for longer than was necessary for someone who didn't drink. What would it matter? A cold glass of Chablis or Sauvignon with his bream ...

Eating alone, it is often said, is a much underrated pleasure. But Frank had been eating alone for so long now he found he had to rack his brains to remember the last time he'd had dinner with someone else. God, that was right, with Brock and his wife, just a few streets from here, nearly two weeks ago.

Rack his brains.

Rockman's – all across the bedspread. Just four weeks ago he'd never killed anything in his life. Never even been hunting. And now here he was, Frank Brill, killer of seven – nibbling a breadstick.

He had regrets about recent events. He'd only set out to kill five. But the dentist's lover. He'd never done anything to Frank. Just happened to be there. Or what about the two guys eating with Beckerman? What was their crime? Just working for or with the NRA? Was that enough? He thought back some years, to the early days of the regime, when 'civility' was being much discussed. What you could and couldn't say online, or in public, and about how all that gradually got eroded. You picked a side and anything was fair game. Until one side got stronger and stronger and showed that they were willing to meet civility with abuse. To meet abuse with fist or club. To meet fist or club with rifle and nail bomb.

'And the sea bass ...' the girl was saying suddenly, sliding the plate onto the table in front of him.

'Thank you,' Frank said.

She noticed the wine list. 'Would you like to order some wine?'

Frank looked at her. 'No, thank you,' he said. 'I'm fine.'

The whole fish on the plate, slivers of herbs and lemon peeping from the slit down its stomach, the row of cherry tomatoes beside it, their skins black and blistered from the grill. 'Enjoy!' she said, marching off. *'Enjoy!'* Just the way he always used to say it, in his tweets.

'I will be interviewed on Fox at 10 a.m. Enjoy!'

And for Frank, reaching again for the cold neck of the bottle of mineral water in the ice bucket, smelling grilling steak and fish, it was time to face the central question.

It was sometimes hard for him to believe, but, in his own tiny way, Frank bore some responsibility for everything, in the same way that a microscopic termite bore part of the responsibility for eventually bringing the whole house down. Incredible and breathtaking as it seemed to him now, there was no getting past his involvement. He'd been a floater all his life. He'd cast his first ballot in the 1984 election, putting his cross against Reagan's name to help give the Gipper his second term, because, well, he came from Indiana and it was Reagan. He'd voted for Clinton first time around but not the second. He'd voted for Obama, twice.

In 2016 he'd been thinking ... what, exactly?

He'd never liked her, that was true. Seemed false. Mechanical. Devious. And also – so smug. Like she knew she couldn't lose. That had irritated folk. It had irritated Frank.

When it came to him, Frank was thinking one thing really. He. Can't. Win. Not possible. But Washington, the

Clintons, the whole machine deserved a good scare thrown up it by seeing this madman get something like 40 per cent of the vote. And then – after the unthinkable happened – Frank thought what a lot of his buddies thought: he'll just play golf and line his pockets and let the people who know what they're doing get on with running things. Well, he played all the golf and he lined his pockets all right. But he did plenty else too. And the guys who were supposed to know what they were doing? Turned out they didn't want to be within a hundred miles of the White House. Frank had never heard the term *kakistocracy* before. He got familiar with it pretty quick.

Oh, it had been crazy, a moment of madness and all that. He'd lost his job. He'd ... Frank had felt like the guy in a bar, getting jabbed in the chest by some other guy who was saying, 'What you gonna do? What you gonna do?' It had felt like the biggest FUCKKKK YOUUUU to that guy. It had felt like headbutting him. But this was ten years ago. Frank had no idea what was around the corner.

So Frank never saw it all coming. What had been meant as no more than a middle finger to government turned out to be a gunshot wound. A butcher knife. A kerb-stomping. Frank felt like those young men in Europe and America in the 1930s and 40s, the ones who joined the Communist Party as a means of protest, as a way of saying 'we believe in a different, a better world', as a way of saying 'fuck you' to their elders. In tiny, minute ways, they had all helped Stalin. Just as in his tiny, minute way, Frank had helped along what happened to America. He'd helped cause all of this: those families sweating on camp beds inside a Texan warehouse, the journalists (like him) who'd ended up beaten and shot, the elderly freezing to death in their homes in winter – in Idaho, in Dakota – because it was pay the heat or pay the medical bills, the journalists, Muslims and homosexuals beaten in the streets every other week now, the Mexican quivering under the thrumming billy clubs, the girl knocked clean off her feet by the snarling truck that mounted the kerb at the protest march, her spine snapped like this breadstick, the kids in the playgrounds screaming for their mothers, trying to hold their guts in while the bullets sang hot around them, his own daughter, falling asleep with a hole in her insides. Frank, and hundreds of thousands like him, had helped all this along. (Wearily, he did the Computations again: *If just a few thousand folk like Frank in key districts had gone the other way, he'd never have been elected, and if he'd never been elected, then Beckerman and Rockwell wouldn't have been able to …*)

He closed his eyes and saw himself in the booth on that November day ten years ago, voting for Trump.

So he did not fear his death. It felt well earned.

When you got towards the end of your life, Frank had read somewhere, you had to fill out a kind of ledger, to do with how you had lived. There will be debits and credits. Most of them, it was said, had to do with love, with how well or how badly you had done by love. Frank thought of his affairs, his betrayals, the hurt he'd caused his ex-wives and his daughter, the awful debits he'd racked up. He had come to a conclusion. He was not a touchy-feely person. He had not come to this conclusion easily, or lightly, it had taken the murder of his wife and son and the death of his daughter to get him there, but he'd got there in the end.

His actions on that November day, Frank now saw, had been an offence, an affront, to love on a par with his betrayals of his own family. All because 'I was pissed off. I never thought he could win.'

Well, he was trying to do right by it now, he thought, looking at the little notepad lying there on the table next to him, the personal and the political, four out of the five names crossed off ...

~~Hauser~~
~~Roberts~~
~~Beckerman~~
~~Rockman~~

Only one name remained.

TWENTY-EIGHT

'He likes to win, you know?'

Chops was trying to understand the sounds of heaven.

Muted, underwater voices, the hum of some kind of machinery, like a rhythmic whirring sound, distant beeps and bings, a metallic clatter of something like cooking pots. He opened his eyes and looked up, bright lights overhead, figures shimmering around him. Were these angels? No, Chops decided as his senses began to return. Definitely not. One of them was a fucking nigger for starters.

'Can you hear me, sir?' The Negro-not-angel was saying.

Chops began to see it all more clearly: the man wore the white coat of a doctor. In the corridor behind him, through the open door, an orderly was cleaning the floor with a polishing machine, the beeping and binging came from the towers of machinery surrounding him, and, over there, on the floor, a nurse was gathering up the cluster of steel trays she'd dropped.

'Can you hear me, sir?'

'Trrrrr ...' Chops growled.

'Listen ...'

'Trrrrr ...'

What was going on with his mouth? His jaw? Chops found that the usual business of speaking had been taken from him. It felt like the left-hand side of his face was made of ice and wood, as though he had been injected with a powerful anaesthetic. He was trying to say 'Yes', but could only produce this 'Trrrrr' sound. He sounded like someone repeatedly trying to start a lawnmower.

'Mr Birner, we –'

'Trrrr ... Trrr ...' Christ this was infuriating.

'You're in Five Palms Hospital. You've been here since yesterday evening. I'm afraid you've suffered a major coronary event followed by a stroke. You were very lucky the paramedics were able to trace your call and find you when they did.'

'Trrrr ...' And now he remembered – the telephone lying a few feet away, somehow clawing 911 into it with the very last of his strength. 'Trrrruuu' – now this was progress! He was managing to add an 'uhh' sound to the 'Trrrr'.

'Please, calm down, sir. You're stable now and we're waiting for some test results to find out how much damage has been done. Is there anyone you'd like us to call?'

'Trrrrruuuuuu ...' Chops gave up, managed to shake his head.

'I'm just going to let the consultant know you're conscious. We'll leave you to rest for now.'

The nurse followed the doctor out and Chops was alone in the private room, sensors taped to his chest, a cannula in the back of his right hand, tubes up his nose. A TV set on the wall was tuned to a local news station. He felt groggy and weak but he found that he could wiggle his toes and fingers, his limbs seemingly unaffected in the way that his face and speech were. What did he remember? The guy, fucking Brill, watching while he choked to death, pointing the gun at him, but too chickenshit to pull the trigger.

Chops tuned into the TV as it switched to a new report: the Florida sun shining across sparkling emerald grass and white sand bunkers. And then a shot of former President Trump, waving to people as he strode along in the familiar chinos, white polo shirt and red KAGA hat. 'And that's the former president live right now in Palm Beach,' the anchorwoman was saying, 'as he arrives at Mar-a-Lago, where he'll be playing golf later today.'

'Still shoots a pretty good game too from what I hear.'

'That's right, Bill. He likes to win, you know?'

Chops smiled – or rather he tried to – as he watched his man, now shouting something to his supporters, giving the thumbs up before he disappeared into the grand building.

Suddenly a jolt of pure adrenalin shot through Chops, causing the twining pale blue lines on the monitor closest to him to ratchet up the screen, the numbers monitoring his heart rate shooting up along with them. He'd seen it, in the apartment. A map of the golf course.

Jesus Christ. Brill was going to ...

Chops looked at the phone by his bedside and imagined the call. 'Trrrrruuuu ...' He imagined trying to explain it to the doctors. 'Trrrrruuuuu ...' No. He had to get there.

He sat up and looked through the glass – no one in the corridor. He stood and took a moment to orientate himself, swaying unsteadily on his feet. As soon as he moved, a couple of the sensors popped off his chest, causing the monitors to start beeping crazily. Chops reached over and turned them off. He crossed to the glass windows facing onto the corridor, drew the blinds and locked the door. Turning to cross the room again he caught sight of himself in the mirror above a small sink – oh dear God.

The left-hand side of his face was frozen in a kind of a rictus grin, more of a snarl really, the lips pulled back from the teeth, the corner of the mouth turned down, the left eyelid drooping down too. He looked like what's-his-face from the Batman films. Two-Face. He looked fucking deranged. He went to speak, in surprise and disgust, and was stunned to hear his own voice properly again as he said – 'TRUUMMMPPPP!'

He tried again. 'Truummp!' Chops said.

And again. 'Trummp?'

This seemed to be the only word the stroke had left him with. That and a face like a melted Marvel villain. This was no time for vanity, however. Chops hurried as best he could – a kind of crab shuffle – across the room to the chair where his clothes lay in a jumble, his scarred, battered heart pounding as he rifled through his shirt and pants. Bingo: his wallet and car keys were still there. He pulled his clothes on and moved to the window, opening it and looking down. Once again his God was smiling upon him. He was on the ground floor. 'Thank you, Lord,' Chops said, the words coming out as 'Truuump, Trrrump, TRUMP!'

Out the window and into the bushes, scratching and cutting himself. Up and across the lawn to a footpath. Even with his slow, crab-scuttle walk it only took Chops six minutes to reach the main road. Another ten minutes until he was able to hail a cab.

'Trruummp!' he said to the driver.

'Fucking A, buddy. Where to?'

'Truummmmp!'

'Yeah, I hear you. But –'

'TRRUMMMMMPPPPP!'

'Jesus Christ, pal …'

Chops got a pen and a receipt pad from the guy and wrote down Frank Brill's address. Seven or eight minutes later Chops was in the parking lot and opening his car door. He checked the glovebox: his spare service revolver and his Oklahoma PD badge were still there.

He started the engine.

TWENTY-NINE

'I just wanted to thank you, Mr President.'

'They sure are thorough,' Frank said, watching.

'Wouldn't want it any other way though, right?' Brock said.

They were standing in the parking lot of the golf course, watching four members of the Secret Service detail search Frank's car. One of them was inside, running a hand down all the seat covers and cracks, looking under the seats, into the glovebox. One was in the trunk, lifting the carpet, examining the well where the spare tyre lived. A third was walking around the vehicle, with a kind of mirror on a stick, using it to look underneath, for a bomb strapped to the chassis, while the fourth stood a little way off, searching Frank's golf bag. He'd already taken out and replaced all the clubs and was now running a hand through all the pockets, rummaging among the tees and balls and markers and old gloves and the ancient, tattered score cards stuffed in there, mementoes in faded pencil of games played with men long dead, matches which had felt so crucial at the time, barely remembered now apart from the odd perfectly struck shot. The wedge hit steeply that arced over a hundred feet in the air and nestled up close to the pin. The well-hit drive, the high draw that followed the treeline and curved soaring around the corner to land in the middle of the fairway. Best of all, the long iron, caught straight out of the socket, travelling two hundred yards and still landing softly, like the proverbial butterfly with sore feet, rolling out into the middle of a distant green — the memories all golfers are left with at the end of their lives. Even now when he stepped onto the first tee it felt to Frank like the possibility of perfection. Like back when he was in charge of the paper and every day would bring the same thing, the possibility of an edition without the bogeys of typos, without poor typesetting, or a badly reproduced photo, or a weak, convoluted opening paragraph, a clunky subheader. It never worked out that way, of course. There was always a fluffed shot. But the first tee, like the blank page, always provided the hope, the opportunity, that this time it would be different.

'Thank you, sir,' one of the agents was saying as his colleague closed the trunk behind him, and a caddy came forward to take Frank's approved, weapon-free clubs off towards the first tee. 'Enjoy your round.'

'Come on,' Brock said, 'we got an hour or so till we tee off. Let's go grab a drink.'

The clubhouse was packed. It seemed like almost every member and their wife had decided to come for lunch that day. There was a palpably different atmosphere from Frank's last visit, almost an electric current running through the place, the sense of a party that was all set to go once the guest of honour arrived.

'Jeez,' Frank said. 'Is it always like this?'

'Pretty much.' Brock laughed. 'Some of 'em just want a picture, a handshake. Some of 'em know that if they get a minute or two they can mention some issue, some legislation they ain't keen on or whatnot and maybe it'll stick and get passed on to the kid, or tweeted about.' They were walking through the busy patio dining area now, heading for the bar, Brock returning various greetings. 'That's his table over there ...' He nodded towards a corner table, roped off, a big umbrella shading it from the morning sun, two secret service agents standing to the side of it, their faces inscrutable as they watched the diners through wraparound sunglasses.

'Do they keep people away from him?' Frank asked.

'Like hell,' Brock said. 'Well, they try. But half the time he just waves 'em on in. Has a chat. Lets them sit down sometimes. You can't tell the big guy what to do, right?'

'You ever done that?'

'Oh sure. A few years back.'

'Really? What did you say?'

'Ah, same as everyone says, I guess. "I just wanted to thank you, Mr President –" he was still in office then of course – "for all you're doing for this country."'

'What did he say?'

'Ah, it was something like "I should do a third term, right?" That was when he was still trying to change that. He should have too. Damn Democrats.'

They got a table near the bar, one of the few remaining, and ordered coffee and water. Here it came, Frank knew, watching Brock pull his chair closer.

'So, how you been feeling, Frank?' Brock asked.

'Ah, so-so. Getting harder to keep any food down.'

'Christ. Doc got you on those anti-sickness pills?'

'Yeah, they make me sleepy though.'

'My buddy Roger said that. You know, you get to our age –' Brock stirred his coffee, sighing, shaking his head, ignoring the close to twenty-year age difference between them – 'you feel every other conversation is about what medication everyone is on.'

'Yeah. You know what? Let's not even talk about it, Brock.'

'No, I didn't mean, shit, Frank, you talk about it as much or as little as you like. Is there anything else you could be doing? How's your coverage?'

'It's good.'

'Because there's a couple of terrific oncologists here ...' He gestured at the rich, white people eating and drinking all around them. 'If you're going to be staying a while I can –'

'Honestly, my guy's great, Brock. But thank you.'

'OK. Well, offer's there. If it's a question of money, I can help you –'

'Seriously, I'm set. But thank you.'

They sipped their coffees. It was strange, Frank reflected, you got them one-on-one, guys like Brock were always generous. When it came to their friends and families there was nothing they wouldn't do for you. But when it came to strangers, especially strangers en masse, it was 'fuck 'em'.

The man sitting across the table from him – like most of the people in this room – wouldn't think anything of sliding Frank, or any one of their buddies, a cheque for ten, twenty, fifty thousand dollars for medical expenses. But suggest putting two cents in the dollar on their taxes to do it for strangers and they'd burn the fucking place down.

Suddenly there was a commotion, people leaving their tables inside and heading out onto the patio as a cheer went up. Frank craned his neck, and turned just in time to see what they were looking at – a flash of white shirt, a red hat, a raised, gloved hand waving as the golf cart sped by the patio, someone shouting out 'We love you!'

'Was that–?' Frank asked, his heart leaping.

'Yep, he's off now. Gonna be about four or five holes ahead of us, I reckon. He plays fast.'

A little less than an hour later the two men stood on the first tee for the second time. 'Right,' Brock said, taking a few preparatory waggles with his driver, 'time to get my money back.'

'Take it away,' Frank said, indicating the tee box.

Brock stepped up and pulled it into the left-hand rough.

'Unlucky,' Frank said.

'For Christ's sake,' Brock muttered as Frank took his place on the tee. He ripped it.

'Shot,' Brock said.

The first half of the round went pretty much the same as it had the last time and Frank was three up when they reached the ninth tee. 'Look out for those trees,' Brock said as Frank teed it up, remembering the one wild drive Frank had hit here two weeks back. Frank set it up to hit his accented fade, the clubface open, the ball far forward in his stance, the club taken back outside the line. He swung hard and – disaster struck. Some golfing sensor built into his hands seemed to detect what was going to happen on the way down and automatically corrected the plane of the swing, bringing the clubface squarely through the ball, sending it screaming off.

'Golf shot,' Brock said respectfully.

Oh shit, Frank thought, as the ball settled in the fairway.

Brock hit his own drive well, down the middle, but a good sixty yards short of Frank's. They rode down in the cart, Frank thinking.

'Shit, I gotta go ...' he said as they arrived at Brock's ball.

'There's a restroom at the next tee,' Brock said, pointing ahead.

'No, I really gotta go, sorry. You know with the ...' he tailed off.

'Oh.'

'Look, I'll take this.' Frank reached into the bag, taking out his rescue club. 'You hit your shot and I'll scoot in there –' Frank nodded towards the trees and shrubs over to their right – 'then I'll hit mine, walk up and meet you on the green.' Brock hesitated, as though he were about to point out that peeing in the woods might be OK back in Schilling, but this was Trump Palm Beach for Christ's sake. Frank headed off towards the treeline at a half-jog. As he reached it he heard the clang of metal on ball followed seconds later by a resigned *'Shiiiiitt'*. He glanced over his shoulder and saw Brock's ball hooking, heading towards the bunkers short and left of the green.

Frank entered the cool canopy of the trees. He looked back towards the tee, trying to work out the line he'd come in on that last time. Panicking now as he tried to locate it, running from trunk to trunk, seeing nothing, just identical trees. What the fuck? What had he been thinking? In the distance he heard the electric whine of the cart as Brock headed off down the fairway, away from him.

And then, out of the corner of his eye, he saw it.

An 'X' carved into the bark.

Frank dropped to his knees and started digging frantically with his bare hands, right beside the roots, getting nothing at first, just handfuls of warm earth and leaves. Then, growing increasingly panicked, he'd felt something hard with the tip of his right little finger. He burrowed harder and got his hands around it.

Just over five minutes later, slightly out of breath, having taken two shots to get on the green, he rejoined his playing partner. Brock looked disgusted. 'What's up?' Frank said, conscious of the extra weight digging into the small of his back. 'Took three out of the trap,' Brock said, defeated.

Once again, Frank won the hole with a two-putt bogey.

THIRTY

'This is America, son.'

Chops cut through the traffic of West Palm Beach. He was sweating, driving fast, terrifying his fellow motorists as they saw the crazed rictus grin coming up behind them in their mirrors, or glimpsed it when he passed them on the right, affording a view of the bared teeth and his insane, fixed expression as he honked the horn and flashed his lights.

As he drove Chops was talking to himself, shouting really, as he tried again and again with his voice, hoping against hope, praying that suddenly there would be a kind of unblocking, like that chunk of McMuffin coming out, and that he'd suddenly be able to speak again. But no. Although there had been an improvement – he was now able to growl the single word 'Trump' with varying degrees of emphasis.

There was an enquiring 'Trump?'

A plaintive 'Trump'.

A surprised 'Trump!'

And a furious 'TRRUMMMMPPPPPP!'

It would have to do, he thought, as he threw a hard left across three lanes of traffic, causing tyres to screech and horns to blare as he pulled into a service entrance of Trump International Golf Club, Chops leaping out of the car and running towards the security booth, leaving the engine running and causing the two Secret Service agents on duty to leap to their feet as he approached.

'Trump!' Chops yelled, gesturing, pointing behind them. They were guarding a pathway that ran off towards the clubhouse, other paths leading off it towards the golf course, the parking lot, etc.

'Yes, sir, the president is here.'

'TRRRUMMMPPP!'

'He's on the golf course right now. But it's members only.'

Chops shaking his head, frantic, pointing at their golf cart now. 'Trump! Trump! Trump!'

The two guys looked at each other – *Jesus. We got a live one here.*

'I'm sorry, sir, we'll have to ask you to move your vehicle. You're blocking this entrance.'

'Mmmm, huuuuuuhh, Trummmp,' Chops said, wagging a finger at them as he ran crazily back to his car. He grabbed what he was looking for and scuttled back towards them, scribbling frantically on the pad as he did so.

'What the fuck is with this guy?' One of the agents, opening the gate and coming round, discreetly slipping the catch off his shoulder holster in the process as Chops thrust the pad at him, the scrawled words 'HE'S GOING TO KILL

TRUMP'. The agent looked up at Chops, looked into the frozen, demented face beseeching him to understand.

'OK, up against the wall,' the agent said, his hand going towards his armpit.

'Don't hurt him, Murray,' the other guy said, Chops seeing him out of the corner of his eye, twirling his index finger around his temple.

Chops realised that it was hopeless, that, at best, they were going to send him packing, at worst lock him up and question him. Right now Brill could be in there somewhere, moving towards the former president, the man who had saved the USA, who had fought so hard and tirelessly against incredible odds and opposition, against the liberals and the deep state and the Democrats and the Lame Stream Media. Who had never taken his salary, who had given his all for his country. A split second was all it took Chops to decide. It was up to him. No one else was going to do it.

He pulled his revolver and shot this Murray in the head, brains and bone and blood blossoming behind him, coppery across the white metal gates.

Swinging the gun around, pushing the barrel between the bars of the gate, shooting Murray's partner twice in the chest as he went for his own gun, the booms of the gun deafening, Chops's ears ringing as he stepped over the dying agent and got into their golf cart. He raced off down a gravel path, following the sign that said 'GOLF COURSE', aware of shouts going up in the distance, off towards the clubhouse.

* * *

At the eleventh, it finally happened.

Frank and Brock came trundling along the cart path to see a small knot of golfers blocking their way, two four-balls, eight guys, all old, dressed in chinos and polo shirts, and, in the middle of them, visible over their heads – the red KAGA hat, the wild pale hair flying out from beneath it. Brock, driving, stopped the cart and asked, 'Wanna go over and say hi?'

Frank swallowed, almost shaking, his voice hoarse as he said, 'Sure.'

'Hey, don't be nervous. He's always real nice. He loves it. Just a quick "hello".'

They approached the gaggle, hearing laughter, seeing now the Secret Service detail hanging back, the two agents wearing windcheaters even in this heat. They looked bored shitless, like they'd done this countless times, even as they cast an eye over Frank and Brock as they approached, seeing just two more rich, elderly white golfers.

Frank could hear his voice as they walked the last twenty yards. Twenty yards. Twenty paces. It took maybe fifteen seconds to cover the ground as Frank heard that roughcast Queens accent, the one he'd been hearing for so long now that he couldn't remember a time without it. The accent was saying 'Hey, they got creamed, and you know what, fellas? They'll get creamed again in '28. If I ran again I'd win again. You know that, right? Right. I'd clean their clock. Even now.'

Off in the near distance, a whine, an electric golf cart at full speed as he went on, 'Ivanka knows that too. She's my baby, I love her. But I kid her. I say, "Baby, you're lucky it's set up the way it is because if I could run again I'd get elected again." Because people – and you all know this, right? – but people are only just realising how popular …' He was signing a golf cap for someone, Frank saw, as they reached the edge of the group. '… I was. Like with Reagan, right? Or Lincoln. The Republicans only know how great someone was after he's gone. But that's, you know, I can take it. I'm tough.' People parted a little, to accommodate Brock and Frank's arrival. A clearing forming, bringing them almost face-to-face. That electric whine, getting closer.

Trump looked directly at Frank as he said 'Right?' again.

Just then the two agents seemed to snap to attention as one, both pressing their fingers to their ears, shoving their discreet flesh-coloured earpieces further in, confusion on their faces as one of them said, 'Say again?'

Frank turned to see a golf cart, about fifty yards away, crashing off the path, coming straight at them and then things seemed to go into slow motion …

Both of the agents drawing their weapons.

One of them shoving Trump to the ground.

The other taking aim at the approaching golf cart.

Frank's jaw dropping as Chops tumbled out of the cart.

He looked crazy, his mouth set in an insane leer, screaming 'TRUMP! TRUMP!' as he brought a gun up and aimed it directly at Frank. All the golfers throwing themselves on the ground, Frank's hand going towards the small of his back as shots cracked in the air, both of the Secret Service guys pumping their triggers, the air moving next to Frank's face as a bullet whizzed past very close to him, Chops seeming to rear back as several bullets hit him in the chest, Frank deafened from the gunfire as he brought the .38 snub nose out and levelled it at the fat old man in the KAGA hat sprawled in the gravel, the agent on top of Trump not seeing him, still firing at Chops, but the other one catching it, swinging his gun around towards Frank, shouting, screaming at him as Frank pumped the trigger now. Then Frank bringing the gun up to his own chin, the muzzle burning his skin even as the agent's bullets hit him first, Frank feeling the shots slamming into his chest, knocking him back and off his feet, sending him over into the lush Bermuda grass beside the cart path.

The things that happened in the final moments of his life.

Birds flying up into the air from the trees behind.

The gaggle of elderly golfers screaming on the ground.

Brock yelling '*OH MY GOD! OH MY GOD!*' right next to him.

The searing pain, blood gurgling up into his throat.

Frank managing to tilt his head a little, looking across to where the agent was back on top of Trump, pumping his chest. The other agent looming over Frank, smoking gun pointed right at his face. It felt like blood was being pumped into the back of Frank's skull now, filling his cranium, streaming around into the cavities of his eye sockets, the blood gradually reaching the corneas themselves, everything darkening, his throat filling, hot and soupy, choking him.

Frank saw something in the grass quite close to him – his little plastic penguin, and on its stomach a thumbprint of blood. The outside world was dimming, although he could still hear it, could still hear men screaming 'Jesus Christ!' and 'Oh my God oh my God', could still feel the distant pressure of the agent sitting on his chest now. The flock of birds in the sky directly above him, black dots wheeling against the blue, the world truly vanishing now, its bright colours being replaced with fizzing images, like the picture on an old cathode TV set as you hopped through many channels, the images all internal, all replays, reruns, old footage, changing from colour to black and white and back again, sometimes sharper, then blurred, frizzed with snowy static, a series of trailers, of highlights unspooling before him –

Frank with the women in his life, with Grace, then Cheryl, then Pippa, at dinner tables, in bars, on hotel beds, in cars, then Olivia and Adam as small children, grass, sunlight, beaches, sitting on his shoulders, climbing on his chest, squealing with joy as he pinched their thighs, tickled their chests, their ribs as small as chicken bones. Frank in the office, in shirtsleeves, grey screens, black text, then black screens, green text, then carbon copies, the methanol smell of the Ditto machine, then at that high school dance, 'Every Time You Go Away', spangled on acid with Robbie that one time out at the lake, the sunset a kind of marmalade that he never saw again. The pressure of that agent on his chest seeming to lessen now, to not matter any more, lifting, moving away as Frank started to become weightless, like he was floating, moving through the agent, beyond him, straining upwards for his place in the universe. Then Frank was with his parents, in the kitchen, his mom doing something at the sink, Frank at the table with schoolbooks as his father came in the back door, in his blue serge overalls, his fingers stained from the ink, the backs of his hands dotted with red burns from the linotype. And the sounds of the world fading even further now and the small child was him, Frank on Schilling main street, in short pants, the cars still finned and chromed, big as great whites, looking up at his mother in a department store, clutching her hand, unsteady on his feet as a new-born colt, looking up at her as she was cooking, him on the kitchen floor now, eating something, a cookie, a piece of bread ('Hank yew, Momma'), not even standing, just sitting up, and then crawling, and then not even that, just gurgling and mewling and kicking limbs. And then he was in his father's arms, in a great national park, on a summer day, somewhere in Indiana, on some rocks, overlooking an endless view, a gorge and pine trees and blue sky and white clouds and huge birds in flight and the vapour trails of jets and a song – 'Paaaper Baaack Wriderrrr' – coming from a radio somewhere, phasing in and out, and Frank knew he was very tiny now, swaddled, and he could smell his daddy – Old Spice and tobacco – and his daddy was saying to him 'Look, Frankie, this is America ... this is America, son ...' and then Frank was feeling sky on his face, the sky brushing past him faster now as he pushed up into it, leaving the gore and the yelling and the screaming way, way beneath him as he seemed to break through the bonds of the atmosphere, brilliant blue giving way to the black icebox of space and then he was safe inside somewhere, somewhere it was soft and wet, a limpid pool, with the sound of a steady comforting thump nearby, a sound he knew instinctively was his mother's heartbeat, the pulse of her blood all around him, and then that was fading too and he was just cells, hunting for each other in the darkness, and then Frank Brill was gone.